PASSION ALLEGRO

Other Books by Ann Ashton

THE LOVELY AND THE LONELY
STAR EYES
CONCESSION
THREE CRIES OF TERROR
THE PHANTOM REFLECTION
THE HAUNTED PORTRAIT

PASSION ALLEGRO

ANN ASHTON

DOUBLEDAY & COMPANY, INC.
GARDEN CITY, NEW YORK
1985

All of the characters in this book
are fictitious, and any resemblance
to actual persons, living or dead,
is purely coincidental.

Library of Congress Cataloging in Publication Data

Ashton, Ann, 1929–
Passion allegro.

I. Title.
PS3561.I417P3 1985 813'.54
ISBN 0-385-19773-X

Library of Congress Catalog Card Number 84-18788

Printed in the United States of America
First Edition

Dedicated to
Osmond Egan

PASSION ALLEGRO

CHAPTER ONE

Tall and slender, with a proud carriage and an air of self-assurance, Mikhail Alexander stepped gracefully onto the stage. Steel-blue eyes, under a slightly unruly mop of nearly black hair, gazed curiously at the assembled audience in the concert hall—a moment of stage fright before he regained confidence and his eyes brightened with a sensuous twinkle that aroused various emotions in those who watched him. Then a smile flashed on the somewhat pouty mouth and the entire handsome face became electric with enticing radiance. Wearing a tuxedo with a black bow tie around his longish neck, he appeared to be fully in command of the situation as he moved to the piano stool and adjusted himself as he sat poised before the keys.

Wavelets of whispers washed through the audience, programs rattled and sighs were heard before a somber hush wafted over the group. Of all the performers at the joint recital, only Mikhail Alexander had received such a stunning reaction even before he raised his hands to the keyboard.

Fingers suddenly danced in lightning arpeggios and clutched handfuls of thunderous chords. His technique was meticulous; his interpretation dramatic; his subtle shadings and bombastic outbursts proved both startling and mystifying. After the opening explosive fanfare, he coerced the keys into a melodic serenade as if he were making exotic love, the piano his inamorata.

Audible sighs could be heard during the ultrapianissimo passages in response to his persuasive lovemaking. He was not stroking the piano keys, but the hearts and emotions of those who were listening. Some were aroused to tears, others responded in more excited ways. Mikhail Alexander was caressing the audience in the palms of his talented hands.

Wide-eyed and lovely, Jennifer Logan sat transfixed by the

magic the young pianist displayed with his brilliant technique and interpretation. Heart-shaped face forward, she felt as if she were sitting on the edge of the seat. Her hazel eyes did not even blink as she observed the performance with utter intrigue and fascination. Heartbeat accelerated, sheer amazement pulsating through her entire body, she sensed the magnetic vibration of the music in every part of her, responding, she imagined, as if Mikhail were actually making romantic love to her, seducing with the skill of the artist that he most obviously was.

Pauline Maples nudged her knee against Jennifer's as the melodic strain charged her with excitement. Not as pretty as her best friend, Pauline still had a youthful beauty and vivacious quality. Like Jennifer, she had been raised largely in private girls' schools and likewise had had little association with young men. The girls had spent many hours in shared contemplation of romantic situations, although actual experience was prudently lacking. Several uneventful dates with boys from a nearby private academy proved to be only modestly stimulating. Cracking voices and metal-braced teeth hardly aroused more than curious excitement; and, since the youths were as inexperienced as the young ladies, such dates produced moderate delight and periodic frustration. The most exhilarating aspects of such charades occurred after they were over and the girls chattered giddily and compared exaggerated notes.

"Of course, they're only boys," Pauline had exclaimed during one such sharing session, "adolescents who hardly realize what it's all about. The jerk I was with didn't know his acne pimples from his elbow. And when he tried to kiss me with a sudden splurge of inexperienced passion, I thought he was going to knock me over. I told him to go home and practice before he tried it again. And he asked, 'On whom?' I could have laughed, and nearly made a suggestion before I remembered my manners. What a drip!"

Jennifer had laughed, since Pauline had a way of amplifying and embellishing a story with the intention of amusing anyone who might be listening. On the other hand, Jennifer had remained silent about the misadventures of her date and accepted the theory that any experience was better than none. Besides, her date for that particular evening, three years ago when she was sixteen, had come from an extremely affluent family and was somewhat more knowledgeable about such matters although he appeared nervous and unsure of himself. Nothing extraordinary happened, but it was a memento to press in the scrapbook of her impressionable mind. Up to now, nothing monumental had occurred in her relationship with the opposite gender. Certainly, she had had the inclination, and the desire to participate in the fullness of love haunted her; she simply had led a much too sheltered life.

The andante passage complete, Mikhail paused a moment before he flew into the allegro section, his hands like jackhammers as they adroitly pounded over the keys, producing a lavish show of technique and fiery interpretation. The effect was exhilarating.

Pauline squirmed and nudged her friend again.

Jennifer's parents were prominent in social circles, and she had been raised with a cultivated appreciation for classical music and the fine arts. Being an art major with promising talent, she often dreamed of venturing into the artist colonies and bohemian groups she had read about. Boyishly handsome Mikhail Alexander reminded her of a young male model who had posed on several occasions for her life-drawing class modestly clad in a posing strap. He had been ushered in by the earthy instructress, Miss Gibson, removed his robe and took the various poses she had directed. When the sessions had concluded, the young dancer, who sat for such classes in abbreviated attire to earn money to continue his ballet training, was immediately robed and whisked off before the girls were permitted to leave their seats. The model, while possessing fine features and a nicely proportioned dancer's body, remained aloof to the situation and appeared just as happy to leave. Miss Gibson later examined the girls' sketchy renderings and tried to be judicious in her opinions of their interpretations, many of which indicated prurient overtones.

The allegro movement soared with resplendent passion, and in Jennifer's mind's eye she imagined Mikhail as briefly attired as the art class model. As the flamboyant strain continued, her fantasies carried her even further into those secret thoughts and speculations that came from having learned the principles in an academic way but having never put them into practice. When her fantasies became as exotic as the music being played, she turned to Margarethe Watts, Pauline's aunt, who had invited her to the recital, and guessed the stately woman was equally enrapt with the performance and her attention held fixed on the dashing young pianist, so that she did not notice Jennifer's reaction.

A patroness of the arts, Margarethe Watts was well known in the artistic circles of Denver, Colorado, where she lived, as well as in similar groups around the country. Extensively traveled and an heiress to legendary wealth, she had periodically sponsored promising young artists in various creative fields. Rarely had she been as impressed with anyone as she was with Mikhail Alexander. She believed it would be a special treat for Pauline and her best friend to attend the recital, which is one reason she had invited the girls to spend the weekend with her. Other musicians on the program possessed talent as well as skill at performing, but none had the charismatic flair of Mikhail. All the technique in the world could go unnoticed without a sense of showmanship, which he possessed.

The last movement was a reiteration of the initial melodic theme this time with variations. The audience reacted with pleasure when Mikhail elegantly wove his fingers over the familiar melody, building it in a fiery crescendo of emotion to a passionate climax, a release of energy that momentarily drained his strength. With three final explosive chords, he lifted his hands from the keyboard and threw his head back before he let it fall limply forward. His body remained erect for a moment to the accompaniment of hushed gasps throughout the audience. Then he rose with nonchalant ease and turned to face his admirers. He nodded more than bowed.

An eruption of applause burst forth in the auditorium along with calls of "bravo" and incoherent exclamations of delight. He nodded time and time again, holding his hands out to his sides and up to acknowledge their acclamation. Then with the confidence of one who has perfectly executed what he had come to do, he turned and left the stage.

Calls for encores rang from the excited throng. He returned merely to applaud the audience but did not go back to the piano. He was recalled a second and a third time. Finally, he condescended to play a short encore which had grandiose style augmented by his flamboyant technique and interpretation.

Again the cacophony of applause and shouting. He remained before the audience for several minutes before he grandly left. The cheering continued, but he did not return.

"It was pure magic!" Pauline exclaimed. She had been the one who had led the standing ovation. "What a dream!"

"Brilliant, isn't he?" Margarethe commented as the house lights came up. "You see why I was so anxious for you to hear him."

"Hearing him was one thing," Pauline gasped, "but seeing him was like 'Wow!' "

"He is remarkably handsome, isn't he?" Margarethe smiled understandingly. "And what was your impression, Jenni?"

"I'm too stunned to speak," Jennifer replied. "He's an amazing talent."

"Don't expect her to sound bowled over by his appearance," Pauline inserted with a teasing laugh. "She never admits that guys turn her on. She pretends she's underwhelmed by them. I could laugh."

"Not necessarily underwhelmed, as you call it," Jennifer defended. "As an artist, I try to be objective."

"Yeah, but how about as an all-American nineteen-year-old girl?" Pauline persisted.

"Your aunt put it succinctly when she said he was remarkably handsome," Jennifer returned. "I think he might be interesting to sketch."

"In the altogether?" Pauline asked, and nudged her playfully.

"Really, Pauline!" Jennifer objected and pretended indignation.

"Ho hum and all that rot!" Pauline grinned in the direction of her aunt. "Jenni likes to put on pristine airs. But anyone who takes life-drawing classes can't be all that blasé. Me, I'd probably draw squiggly lines."

"You're not Jenni," Margarethe stated with a patronizing tone in her voice. "There, of course, is a reception afterward. We could go in and mingle or wait here for a few minutes longer while the crowd thins out."

"You mean with a chance to meet the performers?" Pauline's

expressive eyes widened. "Why wait? I mean, for the sake of culture and all that good stuff."

Margarethe turned her attention to a handsome, well-dressed couple in their middle years. "Mr. and Mrs. Alexander, I'd like you to meet my niece, Pauline Maples, and her friend, Jennifer Logan. The girls, as did we all, found your son most impressive."

Balding and paunchy, Ivan Alexander stepped forward and shook each of the girls' hands. "I am pleased to meet both of you. Such lovely young ladies."

"Yes, we were delighted with his performance," Mrs. Alexander interrupted. "Goodness knows he spends between eight and ten hours a day at the piano practicing. He's so devoted to his music he hardly has time for anything else. But we are proud of him, aren't we, Ivan?"

"Always hoped the boy would follow in my footsteps and go into business," Ivan Alexander said. "Of course, my grandmother was quite a singer in her day. Never made it real big, but she might have if my grandfather hadn't been so conservative. Not at all like his father, my great-grandfather, who was a painter in imperial Russia. Guess that means artistic temperament runs in the family."

"Not in you, Ivan," Mrs. Alexander hurriedly added. She turned to the others. "He's the kind who can walk through a rose garden and ask 'What flowers?' Aren't you, dear?"

"So some people's got a nose for one thing, others for something else," Ivan said. "Me, I can smell out a good business deal. I'm basic down-to-earth, while Constance here likes being pretentious."

"Really, Ivan!"

"There she goes. Come on, let's go in and grab some champagne and get a buzz on before we have to listen to all that gush about Mickey."

"Mikhail," Constance Alexander corrected.

"See, *pretentious.* I wanted to name the kid good ol' American Michael."

"Mikhail was named for his grandfather, Mikhail Alexandrov," Mrs. Alexander announced sweetly to the girls.

"Yeah, and the ol' boy had the good sense to change Alexandrov to plain Alexander."

"Well, I won't hear the end of it until he has some refreshment," Constance stated as she took her husband's arm and led him toward the auditorium exit. "So pleased to have met you young ladies. And, Margarethe, dear, we must have luncheon one of these days soon. So much to chat about. Come, Ivan."

"Ivan is the Russian equivalent of John," Pauline commented as the Alexanders processed up the aisle. "Funny he didn't change his name to John."

"Now, now; be kind," Margarethe suggested with a smile.

Jennifer appeared amused. "Mikhail obviously has his mother's features. She must have been quite lovely as a younger woman. She's still very attractive."

"And Mr. Alexander was certainly a dandy in his youth," Margarethe assured the girls. "Your mother dated him a few times before he fell in love with Constance."

"*My* mother?" Pauline questioned. "I suppose people's tastes —as well as everything else—change."

"He's extremely successful," Margarethe added.

"I can see how that might change someone's tastes," Pauline replied and made a face.

Jennifer laughed.

The lobby was hung with an exhibit of local artists. Most of the audience had adjourned to a large room across from the auditorium where the reception was being held.

A woman of above average height observed from the side of the room. Fashionably attired in a pale lavender suit, she appeared to be by herself and remained aloof from the crowd. Three of the four pianists who had played that evening had put in appearances. She, like most of the others, eagerly waited for the fourth.

"May I assist you with something?" a congenial man with thinning blond hair asked as if he were in some way in charge of the proceedings. "A glass of champagne? God knows there's oodles of everything. I'm Maynard Weiskoff, one of the hosts. You are . . . ?"

"Cleo Dennison," she replied prettily in a melodic contralto. "How do you do?"

Maynard rolled his eyes as if searching his memory. "Cleo Dennison? Has a familiar ring. Have we previously met?"

"I think not."

His eyes widened. "Oh! Not *the* Cleo Dennison with Columbia Artists?"

"*Formerly* with Columbia Artists," Cleo replied, enjoying the recognition. "I'm in business for myself now."

"In Denver?"

"No, New York." She smiled and glanced around. "It was a most interesting concert—as recitals go."

"I'm only a friend of Lionel Adams—a good friend," he said. "I hope you were favorably impressed."

"I've long been an admirer of Lionel's ability to train concert pianists," Cleo stated. "In fact, I've recommended two or three to him for coaching."

"Any of the four who played tonight?"

"No. I had heard of Mikhail Alexander from a former associate who had heard him play six months ago," Cleo explained. "When Lionel sent me word of this recital, and I learned that Alexander would be playing, I made a special trip." She produced a card and thrust it toward Maynard.

"I must tell Lionel you're here," Maynard said, then stopped as he was about to leave—"after I bring your champagne."

Cleo had taken a second sip of champagne when she looked up to see portly Lionel Adams hurrying toward her, Maynard at his side. Lionel wore a tight-fitting tuxedo and a large maroon bow for a tie. Dark-rimmed glasses slipped down his nose, which added to an almost caricature appearance.

"Cleo, my dear!" Lionel exclaimed with a sweep of his hands. "Why didn't you phone or write?"

"I wished for a quiet entrance and to remain incognito during the performance," Cleo replied, turning her face that he might kiss her cheek.

"Maynard tells me you're no longer with Columbia."

"We had a parting of the ways, so I've picked up a few special clients I can successfully push," Cleo returned. "I don't want a large stable. That was the trouble at Columbia, and I had to represent largely who they assigned me. This way I can pick and choose and perhaps better sell those I truly believe in."

Lionel turned to Maynard. "This is honestly a shrewd businesswoman when it comes to artist management. Were I still in the concert-performing end, I'd beg her to represent me." He blinked as he returned his attention to Cleo. "Well, dear heart, what *did* you think of my kiddies?"

"As usual, they reflect your tutelage, which, of course, is a compliment," Cleo stated. "However, I probably don't have to tell you which of them most impressed me."

"Mikhail, of course!" exclaimed Lionel. "He's my prize."

"He has salable attributes," Cleo affirmed. "Do you think he's ready for wider exposure?"

"My dear, is a man ready to make love on his wedding night?" Lionel countered. "Why do you think I sent you the brochure about tonight's fête? Simply because I had one stamp too many? Ridiculous! I wanted you to see him."

"See?"

"He has celebrity quality; he's a performer with a masterful technique. You heard the audience's reaction. He rarely invites friends or family—only his parents, as near as I know—so the response was from strangers. The other three had their own little claques." Lionel wiped a large handkerchief over his brow. "They show promise in their own little ways, but Mikhail is something else. And he's got the artistic temperament to go with it, as well as the dedication and devotion. We play several concertos together—and *he* instructs *me.* I righteously object, of course, but I know he's correct. It's not that I'm slipping, but as you well know, I long ago gave up the notion of being a concert performer. Wait until you meet him—you'll see precisely what I mean."

Each of the three other pianists had groups of people around them offering the usual complimentary praise and encouraging remarks. Pauline and Margarethe had become separated from Jennifer, who had stopped in the lobby to examine several renderings by local artists.

"Hi! Don't suppose you remember me," a young man said as he approached where Jennifer stood appraising a landscape.

She looked up into the eager smiling face, nice features grinning in her direction. There was something familiar about him, but she could not quite place him.

"You probably don't recognize me with my clothes on," he stated and laughed.

"I beg your—" She squinted forward. "Oh, I'm sorry, you're right, I didn't."

"Philip Franklin," he introduced himself.

"The model."

"Actually, I do that as a means of picking up extra money," Philip replied. "And it's excellent training. A dancer has to learn to remain perfectly still, not a muscle quivering or anything. I just set my mind on something remote and concentrate. It's amazing how long one can stand immobile when he has to. You're . . . ?"

"Jenni Logan."

"Just recognized you and thought I'd say hello. My friends are waiting inside. Maybe someday you'll paint me, so my likeness can hang in the lobby here."

"It's a thought." Jennifer laughed.

"We'll talk later—inside." Philip dashed away with the agility of the dancer that he obviously was.

Jennifer stared after him and recalled several quick etchings she had done of Philip—and the comments that Pauline had made when she viewed them. Generally, such sketches in life-drawing lacked distinct facial features, since the purpose was to draw the anatomy. She smiled contemplatively until she returned her attention to the landscape.

As she moved to the next picture, Jennifer had the distinct impression that she was being watched. Had Philip returned? Probably not. She maintained her focus on the watercolor rendering of a delapidated shack in the mountains.

"That's mine, you know," a masculine voice said behind her. "How do you like it?"

It took all the concentration Jennifer could muster not to immediately turn to discover the artist. "I'm impressed."

"A standard, noncommittal reply," the voice stated with a wry chuckle. " 'Impressed' takes a modifier, like 'well,' 'poorly,' 'wonderfully,' 'horribly'—you name it. Watercolors are just a hobby with me anyway."

Jennifer kept her gaze on the painting and tried to make out the scratchy signature in the lower right hand corner.

"I like strawberry blondes," the voice behind continued. " 'Casey would waltz with the . . .' et cetera." He laughed.

She could make out the signature: M. Alexandrov. A chill of excitement ran down her spinal column.

"Did you attend the recital, or did you just sneak in to appraise the artwork?" he asked, stepping closer so that Jennifer could feel the vibration of his aura.

"I—that is—I was at the recital." She slowly pivoted around, practically brushing against him as she gazed up into those steel-blue eyes, now more radiant than they appeared from the stage. She swallowed hard and tried for a smile. She feared it came off lopsided.

"Lovely! Even more attractive from the front," he commented. "Yes, I like."

"Mr. Alexandrov . . . ?"

"That's just what I use to sign my paintings. An old family name before someone back there changed it." His eyes were dynamically radiating into her face. "It's Alexander now—in case you didn't recognize me."

"I—uh—I—that is, I do recognize you," she managed to utter, her throat suddenly dry and her legs trembling. "I—uh—I enjoyed your playing, Mr. Alexander."

"Mikhail."

"Yes, Mikhail."

"And you are?"

"Jennifer Logan."

"And you fell madly in love with my playing?"

"No. I mean, I thought it was brilliant and—"

"Don't give me the 'impressed' bit again."

"Not even with a modifier?"

He laughed, and the vibration of sound thundered through her. "Depends on the modifier, I suppose."

While she searched for an appropriate word, she felt the invasion of his hand about her waist. Her reaction was uncontrollable. Her face paled before it became flushed.

"Come on, let's go some place and become acquainted," Mikhail stated as he applied pressure with his hand.

"But—the reception," she stammered. "People are waiting for you in there."

"Let them wait. They will."

"I'm here with my girlfriend and her aunt."

"They'll wait."

"Maybe getting acquainted should wait." Jennifer finally managed to become a bit assertive. "Don't you care what people think?"

"At the moment I'm only concerned with what *one* person thinks," he returned. More pressure. She began to tremble noticeably. "Easy, baby."

"Please, let's go inside."

"Don't you want to get to know me?"

"Yes, but—"

"I intend to get to know you and I intend to start now." An intense masculine expression changed Mikhail's features as he appeared a man determined to accomplish what he wanted.

"I . . ." Her trembling had become uncontrollable.

"I saw you in the audience," he said in husky throat tones. "You were there in my mind's eye."

"How could you have seen me?"

"I place myself in a psychic trance before I begin to play," Mikhail related as his other hand began moving over her shoulder and up to her face. "Without actually seeing you, your face appeared in my consciousness. It was to your image that I played the exotic love theme as if I were making intense love to you."

"Mr. Alexander—Mikhail, I don't think you should do that," she said as she felt herself responding to his exploring touch.

"Shouldn't do what? See you in my trance?"

"No, what you're doing now. I mean, this is a public place, and it's hardly the proper time."

"Is there a proper time when inspiration strikes?" Mikhail asked, now with a radiant smile that had a tendency to weaken her all the more. She tried to look away, but he held her face with his hand.

"There is a matter of propriety and respect," Jennifer managed to say through quivering lips.

"Okay." His grin widened. "Respect it is."

"Thank you."

In the next moment his lips were touching hers, causing such a burning sensation that she could only respond in one way.

"Relax," he whispered into her mouth. "Don't be so uptight."

"How?"

His lips wove over hers as his hands stimulated her in other ways. "That's better."

"I—"

One more kiss, this time with less intensity, and he gently pulled his face from hers. His eyes blazed deeply into hers. "Okay, let's go in."

Jennifer gasped. She had not expected that reaction.

"You do want to go, don't you?"

"Yes," she replied softly, her body tingling with excitement.

"We'll continue this later," Mikhail said with authority. "A prelude—or, if you will, a preview of coming attractions."

Jennifer stood unsteadily. Mikhail let his hands remain at her shoulders until he was certain she had regained her balance.

"I saw other things in my psychic trance," he said merrily as he pulled her toward the door, "but I'll tell you about those later."

Jennifer swallowed hard and tried to pull herself together.

CHAPTER TWO

The guests were buzzing like katydids on a summer night. Periodic strains of laughter punctuated the din. Most people had had just enough champagne to loosen their tongues and, in some cases, their inhibitions. Both Maynard Weiskoff and Lionel Adams watched the rear entrance from where Mikhail was expected to arrive. Their attention turned to the main door when a buzz of excitement crescendoed and people began to move in that direction.

"My goodness," Pauline all but shrieked as she gazed in the direction of the clamor, "there he is now. And where is Jenni for this big moment? Probably still got her nose stuck in those paintings. The ditz misses all the excitement." She had had sufficient champagne to cause her to slur her words.

"I'm certain Jenni will meet Mr. Alexander—in time," Margarethe assured her. "There's no point in rushing into that melee. We'll have our turns."

When the horde of admirers deluged upon Mikhail like a swarm of descending locusts, Jennifer stealthily pulled back and edged toward the periphery of the crowd. Then she turned in search of Pauline and Margarethe and, not locating them, drifted toward the refreshment tables still in a state of stunned shock at having encountered the dynamic pianist. She picked at the hors d'oeuvre trays, selected three and went to obtain a glass of fruit punch.

"Man, he really attracts 'em, doesn't he?" a familiar voice said at her left. She turned to see Philip Franklin. "Of course, he eats it up—all the attention."

"You sound as if you were a friend of Mikhail's."

"We grew up in the same block," Philip boasted. "He's older than I, but we've been pretty good friends over the years. We were the only two on the block who didn't play the rough games the other kids indulged in. Mikhail was always too preoccupied with the piano and I was busy dancing and getting in shape for same. Naturally, we both got called all the unflattering names that artistically creative kids get. Guess that's why we always stuck together."

"You're very good friends with Mikhail?"

"He's pretty much of a private person," Philip explained, "but I suppose I'm one of his better buddies. He has a place of his own now—out toward Red Rocks, in the boonies sorta. Privacy galore. He has had it well insulated and soundproofed. He likes solitude—especially since he's apt to play at all hours of the night. There's a large studio in his basement that I often use to rehearse in when I feel like making the drive out."

"Then you know him quite well," Jennifer suggested.

"I suppose as well as he'll let anyone know him," Philip replied. "Hey, you're an artist, you know how people with artistic temperaments are."

"I study art and I'd like to pursue it as an occupation," Jennifer replied modestly, "yet at this point, I'm still basically a student."

"In an all-girls' school?"

"My father has never been an advocate of coeducation," she related. "He believes there's too much emphasis placed on social activities and not enough on the scholastic aspect. From what I've seen, I have to agree."

"Must be confining."

"Not necessarily," Jennifer replied. "After all, I've been raised in that way." She thought a moment while Philip scanned the room. "Does Mikhail have any particular girlfriend?" Why had she begun to tremble?

"He dates several." Philip returned his attention to her. "When he has time for them—which isn't too often. Don't know of any he's seeing regularly now. He's had this recital to prepare for and—like I say—he spends a lot of time practicing. Is there any particular guy you go with?"

Jennifer blushed and shook her head. "You might say I live a sheltered existence—which suits me fine right now. I devote most of my time to my studies."

"I'll be in a dance program in a couple of weeks," Philip said as a means of altering the subject. "You'll have to come and see me. With luck, I'll be going to New York next year for advanced studies and to audition for different dance companies. The competition's stiff there."

"So I understand."

Seeing that Jennifer's attention had begun to wander curiously, especially in the direction of the crowd around Mikhail, Philip excused himself on the pretense of wanting to speak with someone in the vague distance. He could not possibly know that she was still recovering from the closeness she had experienced with the pianist, her pulse still racing.

"Nice-looking young man," a voice said at Jennifer's shoulder. "Is he a pianist, too?"

"No, a dancer," Jennifer replied as she turned to face Cleo Dennison. "We've only just met. I know little about him, except that he's a friend of Mikhail Alexander."

"Hmm. Maybe I should have a word with the kid," Cleo speculated.

"Why? Are you writing about Mikhail?"

Cleo threw her head back with laughter. "No, not hardly. I'm in artist management, and if I ever get the opportunity to speak with young Alexander, I'm going to propose representing him in the concert field. The guy's got talent, and personality to go with it."

"Yes, I noticed." Jennifer glanced away.

"Did I say something?"

"No. Just looking for my friend."

"The dancer?"

"No, my girlfriend from school. I think I see her over there. Excuse me."

Cleo tried to read the expression in Jennifer's face before she hurriedly rushed away. Maynard Weiskoff appeared and informed her that he had managed to get a word with Mikhail and he was most anxious to speak with her—as soon as he could tear himself away from his ardent admirers.

"Oh, Jenni," Pauline exclaimed, "I actually got to shake his hand! His very hand! It was all I could do to keep from throwing myself into his arms."

"Really, Pauline!"

"Can you imagine what it would be like to kiss him? Wow!" Pauline's face was animated as she spoke. "Some of the older women went right up and pecked him on the cheek. I've got nerve, I mean, but not that much. And up close, you should see those eyes—steel-blue diamonds. I actually had to look away."

"What do you think it would be like to kiss him?"

"I don't know," Pauline said. "His lips would probably touch mine and I'd faint dead away. I mean, that guy is dynamite!"

"Don't be silly—no one ever faints from being kissed." Jennifer tried for a nonchalant attitude.

"That's easy for you to say. My pulse beat like tom-toms when I shook his hand." Pauline stretched her neck to see what was happening. "Aren't you even going to congratulate him?"

Jennifer stifled a yawn.

"Well, pardon me if I'm boring you."

Within half an hour many of the guests had departed. By then Cleo Dennison had had a chance to corner Mikhail long enough to arrange to meet him the following day for brunch and a business discussion. Once that was accomplished, she said good night to Lionel Adams and departed for the Brown Palace Hotel.

"Looks like the party's about over, girls," Margarethe stated as she arrived where Pauline and Jennifer were standing on the sidelines. "We don't want to be the last to leave."

"I could stand here and stare at him all night," Pauline uttered.

"Stare at whom, dear?" Margarethe questioned.

"Mikhail Alexander, of course. He's such a dream."

"I think it's the champagne affecting her," Jennifer guessed.

"Just because you don't imbibe," Pauline pouted. "You're right, it is time to go home. I need a bed—but I'd appreciate it more if a certain pianist—"

"Pauline!" Jennifer gasped.

"Well, it's a thought," her friend returned.

"We'll say good night to Lionel and his friends," Margarethe said, "then we'll be ready."

"Would it be too impolite if Jenni and I went to the car and waited to avoid all that formal stuff?" Pauline pleaded. Her head had begun to ache and the sparkle had lost its luster.

"Go ahead. I won't be long."

Pauline locked her arm in Jennifer's and pulled her toward the door.

"One moment," a man's voice called from behind them.

Pauline closed one eye as she turned back. "Oh my God!"

Jennifer seemed to freeze in her tracks.

"Jennifer . . . ?" Mikhail called as he stepped toward her. "You're staying the weekend with Margarethe Watts, aren't you? She said you were. I'll call you tomorrow morning. Sorry about tonight, but we'll find time to become better acquainted."

Jennifer nodded her head and jolted forward when Pauline nudged her. Mikhail caught her as she was about to lose her balance.

"Jennifer, is it okay?" Mikhail suddenly sounded like a small, pleading boy.

"Yes."

His hands at her shoulders, he bent forward and kissed her on the lips. "I'll be anxiously anticipating tomorrow." He smiled at Pauline and abruptly turned to leave.

"Oh my God! Oh my God! Jenni, what've you been doing?" Pauline exclaimed. "He actually kissed you . . . Mikhail Alexander actually kissed you."

"Yes, didn't he?" Jennifer was glowing as it was her turn to tug Pauline.

"Why did he do that? I mean, how did he know your name?"

"Questions, questions, Pauline!" Jennifer pulled toward the exit. "I suppose some things just happen."

"Not those kind of things—I mean, not with Mikhail Alexander," Pauline said. "You've been holding out on me."

"Some things are personal, Pauline. Can't you leave it at that?" Jennifer asked.

"I simply can't believe it." Pauline swallowed hard.

Later that night, after she had retired and was stretched comfortably on the bed in one of the guest rooms, Jennifer ruminated about the experience with Mikhail Alexander and her reaction to him. She compared thoughts she had entertained during the recital with those she developed after her initial confrontation with the pianist. Then she considered words Philip Franklin had expressed about Mikhail. Never had she met the likes of the young genius, and most of the youths she had known were far from the creative or artistic types.

She carried fascinated speculations about Mikhail into sleep.

"All right, you have to tell me everything that happened," Pauline commanded the next morning.

"Everything that happened *when?*" Jennifer asked sleepily, since Pauline's invasion of the room had awakened her.

"Oh, don't play naïve with me, Jenni. You know perfectly well what I'm talking about." Pauline thumped down on the bed. "I'll not leave you in peace until you tell me how you met him."

"Who?"

"Mikhail Alexander, of course! Aunt Margarethe says that he's very selective about the girls he shows interest in, although she did hint that he had somewhat of a notorious reputation. He could get notorious with me anytime he pleased," Pauline raved on. "You know, I actually imagined that I was a piano keyboard and he was making beautiful music running his hands over me."

"Really, Pauline, that is private."

"Don't you think I'd tell you every last detail if Mikhail had swept me off my feet the way he did you?" Pauline questioned.

"Brag about it, you mean." Jennifer sat up. "And don't be silly, he didn't sweep me off my feet."

"He certainly impressed you—how could he not?" Pauline bounced on the bed and took another tactic. "Okay, don't tell me. If the excitement were festering inside of me, I'd just have to explode with it!"

"Nothing's festering—nor about to explode," Jennifer assured her, and got from the bed. "What's planned for today?"

"Changing the subject, huh?"

"Dropping it," Jennifer corrected.

Pauline knew when Jennifer made such a statement that she meant it and wild horses could not drag her back on the topic. "Aunt Margarethe said something about shopping. Company's coming late this afternoon for the evening—mostly her music circle friends and a few artists. She assured me that there would be several young guys, so it could be interesting."

"What'll I wear?"

"I think that's why we're going shopping," Pauline replied. "Don't worry, you can put it on Aunt Margarethe's charge card and pay her back later."

"In that case you'd better let me shower and get it together," Jennifer said as a means of trying to dismiss her friend.

Shower water cascaded over Jennifer with a torrent of romantic thoughts and speculations. She soaped her finely shaped body and dreamed, as she often did, of being caressed by a handsome man who knew all the erogenous areas that she had discovered but had never had aroused by someone else. Her fantasies took her on an exotic journey, and the one with whom she was traveling in her imagination was Mikhail Alexander. She wondered how many other women and girls had entertained similar fancies about the stimulating pianist. The number was probably enormous. Even the sophisticated and businesslike Cleo Dennison, with all her reserve and objectivity, undoubtedly had ulterior designs on the young man. Why did she think that? Perhaps it was a look she had seen in Cleo's face when she spoke of Mikhail; or maybe in her imagination Jennifer was convinced that every woman who had attended the concert surely must have had thoughts not unlike her own.

The towel lingered leisurely over her body until she was completely dry. Then she again provoked exotic sensations and contemplations as she soothed body lotion over her soft skin. Although this was a regular practice, never before had she permitted ecstatic mental and emotional reactions as she did while considering Mikhail. Had his music been the motive behind her feelings? Or had it been the close personal encounter with him that had sent her to such heights?

"Jenni! Jenni!" Pauline called as she dashed through the upstairs hallway and came to a skidding halt at the door to the guest room, slippered feet sliding on the highly waxed floor. "The telephone! It's for you. Male and ultra-sexy-sounding, if you know what I mean."

"Can I take it up here somewhere?"

"Sure, in Aunt Margarethe's room."

Jennifer pulled into a housecoat and slippers, wrapped a

towel about her hair and hurried from the room in a flurry of excitement. "Thanks."

"Know who I'll bet it is?" Pauline asked.

"My father."

"Ha-ha! Okay, so you don't want to know!" Pauline called as Jennifer disappeared into the other bedroom.

"Hello." Jennifer gasped to catch her breath.

"Good morning, fair beauty," came the melodious voice from the other end of the line, a tone that had already been ringing in Jennifer's head. "Do you recognize my voice?"

"Mikhail?"

"Good guess."

It was not a guess, but she did not say otherwise. "You said you would call. No one else knows I'm here."

"Great! Then I can have you all to myself," Mikhail stated with his customary air of assurance. "What are your plans for today?"

"Shopping with Pauline and Mrs. Watts," Jennifer replied, bracing herself as she gathered her wits. "Then Mrs. Watts is having a party of some sort this evening."

"Yes, I know. I've been invited," he said. "Can you cancel the shopping?"

"I didn't bring anything appropriate to wear for a party," she returned. "It's a must."

"Oh." Mikhail sounded disappointed. "Okay, then I'll just spend a few extra hours at the piano. I thought perhaps you might have time for that 'get acquainted' session. I'll take out my frustration on the piano—passion allegro!"

"How?"

"A musical term. The best way for me to overcome disappointments is to vent my fury on the keyboard," Mikhail explained. "I've done that ever since I was a small boy. Soon my rage evolves into melodic serenity. I'm accustomed to it."

"It sounds as if your life is a series of disappointments."

"Not at all. Nor is it all rages and dramatics." He laughed. "I'm planning to be there at four. Is it too early?"

"If you arrive before the others, perhaps we can have an opportunity to stroll around and talk," Jennifer suggested. "We're not far from the park and it looks like a beautiful day out."

"Maybe three-thirty."

"Four," she returned with an assertive firmness.

"I bow to your wishes, Jennifer," he returned. "I must remember that all things can't move at allegro pace. I'll look forward to seeing you this afternoon."

"So will I—I mean, to seeing you."

Mikhail had a jolly laugh. "Then since there's mutual desire—"

"Who said anything about desire?" Jennifer questioned, a little annoyed by his presumption.

"You just did. Toodleoo." Silence.

Jennifer stared at the telephone. If she had not known it before, she was unequivocably convinced now that he was a most extraordinary person in more ways than one. She smiled. Her grandmother had always said "Toodleoo." It sounded unusual coming from a person like Mikhail Alexander.

"Well? Who was it?" Pauline asked, unable to curb her curiosity any longer.

"Would you believe a wrong number?" Jennifer teased.

"Oh, come on! I know better than that. It was him, wasn't it?" Pauline persisted.

"Him?"

"Mikhail Alexander."

Jennifer wet her lower lip with her tongue before she responded. "Yes."

"Well?"

"Quite well by the tone of his voice."

"That's not what I meant." Pauline flashed an impatient look. "What did he want?"

"To smother me with kisses and make mad, passionate love to me," Jennifer replied, blinking her eyelids innocently.

"You're kidding?"

"Would I? About something like that?"

"He propositioned you over the phone? Oh my God!"

Jennifer chuckled. "No, I was just putting you on."

Pauline eyed her curiously. "But that's what you wanted him to do, isn't it?"

"Why, Pauline Maples, what a thing to say?" Jennifer put her nose in the air and turned to leave the room. It was all she could do to keep from bursting out with laughter.

Once in her assigned room, Jennifer fell on the bed and hugged the pillow to her, Mikhail's face vivid in her mind.

CHAPTER THREE

When it came to the matter of clothing, Jennifer's tastes tended more toward the practical than the extravagant. She chose simple designs with conservative lines since, more than anything else, she dressed for comfort rather than fashion. Whatever she wore had a crisp look about it, and there was a preference for pastel colors, with occasional earthy qualities about her accessories. Not in the least pretentious, she enjoyed the status of blending into the crowd as often as possible, which actually proved difficult because of her extraordinary beauty, fine features, attractive figure, and the proud yet graceful way she managed to carry herself. Only an experienced eye could detect in her the subtle attitude of a creative artist.

Eyes had always followed Jennifer with curious interest and speculative observations. The strawberry blond hair had a way of punctuating her presence like a passing flame, arousing attention, a fact to which she was oblivious—and a condition which nearly drove Pauline Maples to the brink of distraction.

"Can't you see how people ogle you?" Pauline would ask when they went out together.

"What people?"

"Well, practically everyone. And those who appear to be unobservant secretly catch glimpses out of the corners of their eyes," Pauline exclaimed. "Me, they take ganders at and make unflattering faces. Mom always said I had a puss only a mother could love—and sometimes she has difficulty."

"You're making that up."

"Am I? Wish it were true. You, on the other hand, could make a marble statue smile with salacious interest."

"Come off it."

"Wait till we pass the next statue—and I don't mean those in an art museum. *That* could get downright embarrassing."

Jennifer often laughed at Pauline's outrageous remarks. She always encouraged her with flattering comments, aware that Pauline was envious of her natural beauty.

"You know, if you were to choose a real sexy creation," Pauline said that day, "you'd knock the eyes out of everyone."

"I have no desire to disrupt anyone's vision," Jennifer returned. "I just try to be me. If that attracts attention, there's really nothing I can do about it. But, goodness knows, I don't let it bother me. Everyone has a right to his own opinion."

"Easy for you to say," Pauline remarked. She did not always hide her envy of Jennifer's beauty, but she tried to accept facts as they were.

Predictably, Jennifer chose a simple yet dressy outfit, solid lime green trimmed in white. The color accentuated her reddish blond hair and an emerald quality in her eyes. On the other hand, Pauline went for a creation with ruffles and somewhat daring lines. She had a large bust, so she selected a low, revealing neckline.

"So they don't get impressed with the face," Pauline said, "let them look a little lower and become turned on."

The shopping expedition, including luncheon at a posh restaurant, took until two-thirty. When the shoppers returned to the Watts home in a particularly elegant section of Denver, Jennifer excused herself to nap for an hour.

Sharply tailored in gray tweed, with just the right touches of feminine accessories, Cleo Dennison waited in the lobby of the Brown Palace Hotel at precisely noon. Always punctual, and insistent upon that trait in her clients, she checked her watch with the hotel clock before she took a seat with a clear view of the front entrance.

At three minutes past twelve Mikhail Alexander pushed merrily through the revolving door. Dressed casually in sports attire, he surveyed the lobby before examining his wristwatch. By the time he looked up, Cleo had crossed to where he was standing and greeted him with a large smile.

"I'm glad to see you're on time," she said. "Punctuality always scores points with me."

"I don't know about scoring points," Mikhail returned. "I happen to believe in being prompt."

"I must say you look particularly handsome today," Cleo commented as she swept her eyes over him. "Yes, indeed. I would say you have many salable qualities."

"Salable?" Mikhail grinned. "I'm not for sale."

"I didn't mean it in a crude way, naturally. But you are an amazing concert artist—and someone with handsome good looks is far easier to promote than one with less attractive features."

"Men like Beethoven would cringe with disgust at such a statement," Mikhail said, "since he had a case of the uglies. Still, his personal appearance didn't affect his artistry."

"Perhaps it did," Cleo countered. "If he had been a remarkably handsome man, he might have been more of a socialite—a playboy, if you will—and not have devoted so much of his time to being creative."

"I'll accept that as your opinion, although I don't necessarily agree with it," Mikhail replied. "I believe if a person has talent and an artistic temperament, his creativity is quintessential to his entire character. What people think of my appearance is hardly important to me; what they think of my playing *is*."

"Spoken like a true artist," Cleo remarked as she motioned him toward the hotel restaurant. "I've reserved a table."

Mikhail politely followed her lead.

"I made several important phone calls this morning," Cleo stated after they had ordered. "I've already generated a little excitement about you to some of the right people. Once I get back to the big city, I'll make other valuable connections. I've several very wealthy contacts, people who sponsor young artists."

"Patrons?"

"Basically, they're supporters of the musical scene, philanthropists who perpetuate the arts," Cleo explained. "What I will want to do is arrange for you to perform in concert for a select group, possibly in a small concert hall. If you can arouse interest in them with your exceptional talent, I'll move in with a heavy selling job to acquire their support. When that is accomplished, plans will be made for your first public concert—probably at Carnegie Hall."

"Does that mean I'll have to live in New York?"

"Possibly—at least be there for extended periods of time."

"What do you get out of this?" Mikhail asked after studying her businesslike expression.

"Until you become established, I'm simply gambling with my time and energies," Cleo replied. "As agent-manager I usually get twenty percent of what you make. If I have to go through another agency, I split my fee with them. Don't frown. Many managers charge as much as twenty-five percent and agent fees are above that. Like I say, I'm taking a gamble—because I believe you have tremendous talent and that you can be extremely promotable. A person in my capacity takes a lot of risk with a totally unknown newcomer."

"I can appreciate that," Mikhail said as he studied her face. "Just out of curiosity, how do you survive taking such chances on people like me?"

"I have three artists who are doing fairly well in the concert field," she related, "and I do have my own sponsors who underwrite me. Lacking it in myself, I appreciate excellent artistic talent."

"Do you really have so much confidence in me?" Mikhail asked modestly as he attempted to discern if there were ulterior motives in Cleo's expression.

"I've covered hundreds of concerts—especially like the recitals Lionel Adams gives," Cleo continued. "I hear many students with much promise—but they are precisely that, promising *students.* Rarely, as in the case of last night, I discover a performer who has moved beyond the student category. And, like Lionel, I believe that you are ready to become a professional. Ergo, I have invited you here today."

"Are you sexually attracted to me?" Mikhail candidly asked.

Caught off guard for a moment, Cleo paused to gather her wits. A tongue to her lower lip before she smiled, then, staring deeply into his eyes, she replied, "I'm a perfectly normal woman with sexual instincts and drives. I would be lying if I told you I didn't find you enormously sensually attractive. However, I am also several years older than you and, undoubtedly, more mature than you in many ways. I've long since learned that one does not successfully mix business with pleasure. I also realized that practically every woman in the audience last night entertained romantic speculations about you. That is an asset for you, if you use it as such."

"Meaning?"

"Think about it." Cleo sipped from her water glass. "Celebrity performers who make it big, whether in the concert field or in popular music, all have a certain sexual charisma which they project. That's the name of the game in this day and age. And I suspect it has always been true to one degree or another. The secret is not to mix your personal life with your professional life. Learn to remain aloof from your public. Let them dream, desire and want—romance them with your music and you'll cultivate a throng of followers. Learn that, my young beauty, and you will go far with your career. Become careless and let your private life interfere with your professional, or allow your professional life to intrude on your private, and you'll be courting trouble. Remember that and you'll do just fine."

"Okay, I'll buy that. What happens now?"

Cleo removed papers from her bag. "Here's a contract, an agreement between the two of us. I want you to look it over. If you feel it necessary, have an attorney examine the contents. In any case, have Lionel Adams go over it with you. I'll be flying out of Denver tomorrow evening. If you decide to sign, you can reach me here at the Brown Palace. Once signed and witnessed, we'll be in business, and I'll be off to New York to put arrangements into motion."

"I appreciate your interest, your candor and your advice," Mikhail stated as he took the papers. He reached to squeeze her hand. "My dad isn't the least bit artistically inclined, quite the opposite, but he is a businessman. I'll have him check out the contracts with me."

"I believe in you, Mikhail. Don't let me down."

Upon leaving the Brown Palace, walking slightly on air, Mikhail called Philip Franklin. "I need to talk."

"I'm going to the Watts' party this afternoon," Philip replied.

"Me too. Let's talk, then go together."

"Sure, why not? Give me an hour."

"Okay. I'll have time to dress."

Rather than drive all the way out to his house near Red Rocks, Mikhail went to his parents' home, where he had left a suit. While there he showed the contract to his father. The elder Alexander thoroughly scrutinized it.

"You're really serious about this business, aren't you?" his father asked as he put the papers aside.

"You know it's the only thing I've wanted to do since I can remember," Mikhail returned.

Ivan Alexander gave a dyspeptic look to indicate disapproval. "Can't say it's right, can't say it's wrong. The dang piano has been alien to me. I don't understand it or musicians. I only know business and how to make money. I'm disappointed that you've chosen such a profession, but since you have, then I'll support you as best I can. Suppose this means your mother will be haulin' me off to New York and God only knows where to hear you play."

"What about the contract?" Mikhail questioned.

"Looks good to me." Ivan glanced down before he forced a smile and extended his hand to his son.

Mikhail shook his father's hand, then impulsively stepped forward to embrace him, holding him tightly and kissing him on the cheek.

"With strength like that," Ivan said, "you could be—"

"A fantastic pianist," Mikhail filled in.

"That wasn't precisely what I had in mind, but it'll do."

"Will you witness my signature?"

Ivan considered the question before he consented.

After leaving his folks' house, Mikhail went to pick up Philip, and the two drove around and talked for nearly an hour before they went to the home of Margarethe Watts.

"Aren't you excited?" Pauline asked when she invaded Jennifer's assigned room. "I mean, aren't you just about going mad with anticipation?"

"Of what?" Jennifer casually asked as she put finishing touches to her makeup and hair.

"Of *what?* Jenni Logan, you're abnormal!"

"Not in the least. A party's a party. Right now I'm concerned with looking my best," Jennifer replied. "I really like this outfit."

"You could have chosen something more startling and alluring," Pauline opined. "If Mikhail Alexander were coming expressly to see me, I'd string a few fig leaves together and that would be it."

"Really, Pauline! I won't dignify that remark with a comment." Jennifer continued her attention at the mirror.

"Aunt Margarethe said she invited some guy by the name of Philip Franklin—a dancer or something like that. She said she pointed him out to me last night. I don't recall. Couldn't have been very impressive."

"You know those sketches I did in life-drawing class?"

"You mean the faceless wonder with the 'oh, wow' bod?" Pauline questioned.

"Philip Franklin was the model."

"You're kidding!" Pauline suddenly became animated.

"You nearly fell off your perch when you first saw the sketches of Philip."

"Yeah—even without seeing his face." Pauline thought a moment. "Ugly?"

"Quite the opposite."

"Then why didn't you draw his face?"

"Wasn't time." Jennifer enjoyed watching Pauline's reaction.

"Do I look okay? I mean, are the ruffles in place and all that good stuff?"

"You look great."

"How could I possibly?" Pauline dashed from the room with the intention of revamping her entire appearance.

Jennifer laughed. Then her expression changed as she examined her features. Why wasn't she as excited about seeing Mikhail Alexander as Pauline thought she should be?

"Maybe if you decide to take a place in New York," Philip said as they arrived at the Watts' house and Mikhail pulled the car into a parking spot, "I could come and share bachelor quarters with you until I'm situated."

"Always a possibility—*if* I'm still a bachelor by the time you arrive in New York—and *if* I take a place there," Mikhail returned.

"Huh? You thinking about getting married?"

"It's a consideration," Mikhail replied. "Particularly after my chat with Cleo Dennison and her advice about not mixing business with pleasure. I mean, what would be more practical?"

"Do you have someone in mind?" Philip questioned as he pushed the car door open.

"No one definite—yet. But I may soon." Mikhail laughed as he stepped from the car and slammed the door. "After all, I'm twenty-five, and I've sown enough wild oats to want to settle down and think seriously about the future."

"With a possible concert tour ahead of you?"

"It could be a protective measure," Mikhail allowed as they went to the front door.

Philip reserved comment.

Margarethe Watts opened the door to the two young men and warmly greeted them, explaining that the catering people were just setting up and the man who was to act as butler was occupied. "Besides, I wasn't expecting anyone quite this early."

"I told Jennifer Logan that I would be here ahead of time," Mikhail said. He was wearing a light tan suit, brown shirt and beige tie, an outfit that emphasized his tall, slender, majestic body. His eyes danced with excited anticipation.

"I don't know that Jenni is ready," Margarethe returned, trying not to appear bewildered. "Why don't you and Philip go into the sitting room and I'll check with her?"

"Thank you."

"Mr. Alexander," a voice called from the top of the stairs.

Margarethe turned back as she saw Jennifer descending the steps. "In that case, perhaps I should rouse Pauline to come and amuse Philip."

Jennifer extended her hand to Mikhail, then to Philip as she smiled sweetly at each. "It's good to see you both again."

"Our pleasure," Mikhail replied, speaking for Philip as well. "It was convenient for Philip to come with me. But I'm certain he'll excuse us while we go for that walk we had mentioned."

"Perhaps we should wait until Pauline arrives," Jennifer suggested.

"No need," Philip stated. "I can relax and wait."

Mikhail reached for her hand as Margarethe hurried up the stairs. He winked at Philip before he gently tugged Jennifer toward the door.

"He's really very nice," Jennifer commented as they walked out into the fresh afternoon air with just a touch of autumn to it. "Perhaps I should have brought a sweater."

"I'll see that you're kept warm," Mikhail returned with a large smile that implied much. "You were speaking of Philip?"

"Yes."

"We grew up together. Since each of us was an only child, we're practically like brothers," Mikhail said. "You're an artist, aren't you? I mean, Philip said he had posed for your life-drawing class."

"Yes. He's a very good model."

"Maybe I should pose for you sometime," Mikhail offered.

"Only if it's in life-drawing class."

"Why?"

Jennifer felt as if she had begun to blush. "It would be prudent."

Mikhail laughed. "I'd hardly take you for being overly prudish. I mean, most artists I've known have a very liberal attitude toward life and the human experience."

"The human experience?"

Again he laughed. "I think you pretty much get the picture."

"In that case I will have to admit that I am *not* like other artists," Jennifer stated firmly. "The fact is, the only would-be artists I've known have been fellow students—and most of them have taken art courses because they're relatively easy."

"I'd like to see some of your artwork," Mikhail said, undaunted by her remark. "The fact is, I'd like to get to know you much better."

"That's curious," Jennifer replied, realizing that she needed to mellow her attitude. "I was thinking I would like to know you better. You strike me as being quite worldly wise, and I have to admit that mine has been a rather sheltered existence."

"Always private girls' schools?"

"Always."

"You must entertain a lot of unfulfilled fantasies," Mikhail suggested. "I mean about many things."

"I've read a lot."

"Reading and doing are two different things."

"Yes, I know."

They had reached a wooded area at the edge of the estate. Mikhail suddenly stopped as he held firmly to her hand. As they faced each other, he put his other hand to her face.

"You're absolutely beautiful, Jennifer, absolutely," he said softly. "I'm completely fascinated."

"Mikhail . . . ?"

"Do I overwhelm you? I hope so."

"Why?" She was trembling as his face moved closer to hers.

Mikhail smiled as his eyes penetrated into hers before they focused on her mouth. In a moment their lips were touching. She reacted with alarm at the electric sensation, then her lips softly parted and her hands reached to embrace him as wave after wave of passion moved through each of them, exploding with fire.

CHAPTER FOUR

"I can't believe this is happening," Jennifer gasped as her lips pulled away from Mikhail's, and she could not resist allowing her body to lean into his. Each nerve end seemed aglow with magnetic response, every fiber of her being stimulated by the insistence of his touch, his exploring caresses, his vital strength, artistic yet so very masculine. She wanted to scream with delight and, at the same time, cling to the massive protective aura that exuded from him.

"Believe it, Jennifer, because it *is* happening," Mikhail said softly as his lips brushed against her ear.

She pushed her cheek against his. "I've never experienced such sensations."

"And this is only the beginning," he replied as his lips kissed from her ear, over her cheek and again to her mouth. "I have plans for you."

"You have?" Her lips barely touched his as she spoke.

"Many, many plans," he returned. The intensity of the gaze from those steel-blue eyes riveted through her. She felt he must be staring into her soul.

"Wh-what plans?" She trembled with a crescendo of anticipation. When he continued to stare and say nothing, she could no longer restrain herself. One hand at his back forced him closer, the other hand at his head pulled it down to hers until no space remained between them. Lips apart, she accepted the full thrust of his passion. Sparks of electricity seemed to be crackling around them, explosions of emotion that erupted with soul-consuming desire.

"Easy, baby, easy," Mikhail whispered, lips moist as they caressed her cheek. "Certain things need to progress slowly—we need more of a prelude to the main theme. It makes it more exciting that way. In some pieces of music, a composer spends an entire movement in preparation for the principal melody."

"Can you equate musical composition with making love?" she asked, stinging lips barely able to form the words.

"Naturally. I am convinced that most composers were incurable romantics," Mikhail stated, still tightly embracing her, but easing the intensity of his muscular reactions.

"I realize that music often expresses emotion," Jennifer managed to say, although the excitement surging through her body made sorting her thoughts difficult.

"When I play a sonata, for instance," he remarked, still holding her tightly to him, "I envision the emotion and feelings, the absolute passion the composer must have been experiencing at the time he wrote it. Yet as I interpret the piece, my fantasies explore definitions of what those emotions must be according to my awareness. On the other hand, should I be playing a fiery polonaise, I put myself in the mood of the piece, pictures of triumphal conquest ablaze in my mind."

"Physical conquest?"

"Eventually, all emotions evolve into physical release in one way or another," Mikhail stated with a soft chuckle that vibrated through her. "Even when I play themes that reflect solitude and contemplation, invariably I feel the romantic undertones of longing and desire. Why would a composer write a melancholy piece if he were not lonely for the expression of emotional fulfillment? And I can certainly relate to that."

"You amaze me," Jennifer commented and reached her face to his for another taste of his mouth.

"You rather amaze me, too," Mikhail replied after he had kissed her. "Creative artists have such a delightful passionate response."

"I've never—"

"Oh yes. Would you be insulted if I told you that I realize you're inexperienced in certain things?" he asked as he gently stroked her hair.

"How can you tell?"

He laughed. "Intuitively, perhaps, or merely because I perceive that is the case. You delightfully follow my lead—which I appreciate—but a woman of greater experience would react differently."

"Have I disappointed you?"

"Not in the least, my dear Jennifer, not in the least," Mikhail said. "You're so very refreshing—a challenge."

"Why a challenge?"

Mikhail thought a moment before he released his stout embrace and reached for her hand. "We were going for a walk, weren't we?"

"Are you upset?" She held tightly to his hand.

"No, not at all. Prelude, remember?" Again laughter.

With the absence of his arms around her, Jennifer began to notice a slight chill in the air. They walked close and she felt flushed with an inner heat, yet she wanted more physical contact. In those following few moments, she was able to gather her wits and realized that she had let her fantasies carry her away. Was it wrong? She recalled words of wisdom from a favorite teacher who had warned that it was far better to entice and leave a man wanting than to submit immediately to his insistent advances.

"My father would have liked me to go into business with him," Mikhail said as they turned in the direction of the park. "I can understand his concern. After all, I am his only child. I've taken a few business courses, and I suppose if I applied myself, I could eventually assume a business position with him."

"I couldn't imagine you as a businessman," Jennifer stated, now more in control of her physical reactions. "You're such a splendid pianist and really a marvelous interpretive artist."

"Thank you for saying so," he returned, and squeezed her hand. "That is what I want to be. Actually, I took several art classes, especially watercolor and design. I always figured I could fall back on doing architectural renderings for contractors if worse came to worst. Consequently, I do a few watercolors for my own amusement. It gives me diversion and an excuse to stay away from the piano. Then, too, I have aspirations toward becoming a composer. I've written quite a few pieces, and eventually I'd like to get heavier into that aspect of music. It'll mean more formal training and studying with composers—but that will come in time."

"You're absolutely fascinating."

"Are you referring to my ambitions?"

"Yes, *that*, too."

"Implying that you find me fascinating in other ways."

"Yes."

"Such as."

"Objectively, as an artist, I think you're beautifully proportioned," Jennifer said, uncertain how it sounded. "I mean you have extremely handsome features."

"Thank you. Objectively, as an artist, I think you're quite lovely—pretty face, alluring body." He smiled as he observed her. "But subjectively?"

"Subjectively?" Jennifer swallowed as a dryness came to her throat. "I was trying to be objective."

"I know—but I sense you were really being subjective."

"Possibly." She turned away and pretended to look into the distance. "I love the coming of autumn."

"So do I—even if you are attempting to change the subject." His laughter rumbled through her and she smiled in reaction. "What's on your agenda for tomorrow?"

"I haven't discussed plans with Pauline and Mrs. Watts."

"Need you?"

"I am their guest."

"What if I invited you to see my house out toward Red Rocks?" Mikhail asked.

"Objectively or subjectively?" she quipped.

"That will be entirely up to you," he said. "I want to show you my world, my home, the way I live."

"Why?"

Mikhail stopped and turned toward her. He caught her other hand in his. "Because I like you—I like you very much."

"You mean you like my appearance?"

"I suppose that comes first, doesn't it?" He chuckled as he gently tugged her forward. "There must be a physical attraction—and believe me, as far as you're concerned, that is in the positive. But what really appeals to me is the inner you, your personality, your artistic sense, even your shy, somewhat conservative manner. When a girl is too eager and comes on too strong, the challenge is gone."

"Challenge?"

"I like challenges," Mikhail explained. "When I open a piece of music for the first time and gaze at all those black notes, it's almost like looking at a book written in a foreign language. But I accept the challenge, read through it, begin to work out the complex fingering and eventually memorize it. That process may take several weeks, but eventually I make it a part of me and begin interpreting it according to my own emotional response. It's a challenge and I conquer it—but not without time and effort. A girl, on the other hand, who is too easy, never really becomes a part of me. We may make out like champs, but it's all exterior, superficial. I don't really know her and she doesn't know me: the proverbial ships passing in the night. Maybe what I'm trying to say is that I'm looking for substance in a relationship, substance that will become an intricate part of my life."

"And you think I might have those qualities you're seeking?"

Mikhail stopped again as they reached the entrance to the park. "It would be nice if you did. What I've discovered so far appeals to me."

"Can't you have your choice of practically any woman who hears you play?" Jennifer asked as she looked away to avoid his intense gaze.

"When I was emerging from puberty, I thought, like all other pimply faced youths, that one conquest after another was the name of the game," Mikhail confessed. "Believe me, I played the game—but it was only that, a game. Perhaps it's a sign of maturity, because now I want a helpmate as well as a playmate, someone with whom I can share the many aspects of my life as well as theirs. Sex is the cherry on top of the whipped cream on top of the frosting on top of the seven-layer cake—not the cake itself, if you know what I mean."

"I had a teacher who once made a similar observation," Jennifer replied. "I'm beginning to perceive what she meant."

Again those steel-blue eyes penetrated deeply into hers. A tongue over his turgid lower lip made it glisten as he lowered his face to hers. "I have a good feeling about you—about us, Jennifer." His arms had encompassed her, and she reached out to touch him, becoming ignited by the sensation of coming into close contact with him.

"I've never been so—I mean, this has never happened to me before," she stammered. "It's all so new."

A soft breeze arose, tumbling dry leaves across the browning grass. Jennifer and Mikhail held tightly to each other, their mouths together, their hands stimulating, their bodies tingling in reaction. The force of Mikhail's physical intrusion inundated Jennifer with liquid desire until she could not help but respond fully. She did not think right or wrong, she only perceived beauty as her emotional response soared to match what was happening in her physical being. She wanted—at that moment she wanted him, the full force and impact of him; she desired to be a complete part of him. A scream began in her solar plexus, a scream of delight that wanted to erupt with ecstatic sound.

"Mikhail! Mikhail!" she said softly, but to her it sounded like a scream. "You can't know what you're doing to me."

"Oh, but I do," he whispered, aware that the fire in each of them was blazing with the fury of a furnace. He held her face to his chest as he raised his head and let the breeze bring a sobering effect to his face. Still, his arms tightened with such power that he feared he might crush her with the might of his passion. Gently, methodically, he began to stroke her hair and let his hands run down over her back. He continued holding and caressing her as if he understood what she was experiencing and how alarming it must be for her. Why shouldn't he know? He, too, had been sparked with a corresponding reaction.

"Have I disappointed you?" she asked as he decreased the intensity of his embrace. Then he caught her face in his hands, those majestic fingers that coaxed elegance from the piano keyboard, and, as his thumbs outlined her lower lip and chin, he kissed her with compassion and gentle understanding.

"Oh no, Jennifer, you've not disappointed me, very far from it," he sighed. "I am abundantly pleased."

"I hope so."

"Do you? Why?"

"Because I am pleased."

Mikhail kissed her again, still cupping her face in his hands.

"In that case I think it would be judicious of us to return to the party."

"Because you're anxious to be there?"

"No. Because I fear if we continue as we've been doing," he assured her, "matters could go too far. Just because the cherry is on top of all the other goodies, doesn't mean we have to get to it first. Fact is, I prefer saving it for the last."

"Can we wait a few minutes?" Jennifer asked. "I'm trembling so much, I—"

"Okay. I comprehend. I need to relax a bit, too," he said. He took her hand.

From the distance came the scent of burning leaves. Squirrels scampered in acorn-gathering rituals, stopping only briefly to eye the young couple.

"Where is your school?" Mikhail asked a few minutes later as they left the park.

"Out near Boulder," Jennifer replied. "It's rather remote and isolated on a large estate. The buildings are old. Allegedly it was once the home of a silver baron. When he passed away, his family arranged to turn it into a private girls' school. It had something to do with the bottom falling out of the price of silver and a need for them to survive. The original family lives elsewhere."

"How did you happen to choose that particular school?"

"My mother was raised at Larchmont—that's the name of the school," Jennifer replied. "My parents are quite conservative, with very definite moral ideas. In a way, I feel a little deprived not having experienced a public education. Still, when I read about all that goes on in such places, Larchmont gives me a feeling of protection."

"Are you so insecure?"

"Hardly." She laughed and squeezed his hand. "I've had a thorough education and I'm really fond of the sequestered life at Larchmont."

"When do you graduate?"

"I graduated last June," she returned. "I simply returned to take additional art classes because I'm fond of the instructress and I really didn't want to go on to a university—and the thought of going to an art school terrified me a little."

"Why's that?"

"Because I suspect it's a way of life that is completely alien to me," Jennifer explained. "I've practically led a cloistered existence at Larchmont. I've read a lot, and Pauline has regaled me with stories about the wild and wicked world out there—especially among the unconventional artists and that type of person."

Mikhail sounded amused. "And what does Pauline know about such things?"

"She has a brother who's an artist," Jennifer continued. "She's met a lot of his friends and overheard their stories. Things she told me practically curled my hair. Okay, so I'm really terribly naïve about a lot of things."

"Are you afraid that if you get out there among the other artists, that you'll become like them?"

"I don't know. I might. I guess I have a lot of repressed desires—although I don't believe I could pull out all the stops and live a life of utter abandonment. I mean, I do have principles."

"But you're curious," Mikhail stated. "And that curiosity just might lead you to explore various avenues of adventure."

"Possibly. I suppose you know all about that."

Mikhail thought a moment. "In a limited way. I guess I've heard all the stories, too. And I will admit that I've done some experimenting along the way. In the end the novelty wears off. Being one of the gang can be time-consuming and not particularly productive. Guess I've got built-in motivation for success."

"You certainly have what it takes to make it," Jennifer remarked, and again squeezed his hand.

"That's why I have to get my personal life together, my act, as they say," he commented, "and move forward with what I want to accomplish."

Several questions entered Jennifer's mind, but she declined to ask them. Instead, they walked in silence back to the Watts' house.

Most of the guests had arrived by the time the young couple returned. Prominent among them was Lionel Adams with Maynard Weiskoff. Many faces appeared somewhat familiar to Jennifer, since they had been at the concert the night before.

"Here's the dear boy now!" Lionel exclaimed as he swept

Mikhail away from Jennifer, leaving her slightly bewildered. "I've scads of people for you to meet. And, of course, everyone is talking about you, Mikhail, absolutely the entire of Denver."

Jennifer observed, and drifted to the sidelines.

"Well, what happened?" Pauline quizzed as she pounced on her friend.

"What happened when?" Jennifer found the question annoying.

"Just now with you and Mikhail Alexander," Pauline persisted.

"We took a pleasant walk to the park, watched the squirrels and got acquainted," Jennifer said, trying to affect a nonchalant attitude.

"Did he try anything?"

"Try what?" Jennifer blinked innocently.

"Oh, Jenni, what ails you?" Pauline asked, showing perturbance. "Had it been me, I would have pulled him into the bushes and—"

"Really, Pauline, you can be most adolescent at times!"

"Well—?"

"No bushes." Jennifer surveyed the room. "How'd it go with you and Philip Franklin?"

Pauline shook her hand to indicate that she was unimpressed. "He's nice-looking and all. But he's no tiger, if you know what I mean. I could have laughed. Well, not really. I mean, what do I know about dance—I mean, classical stuff like ballet? The vibes just weren't right. Then some of his friends came, and he dragged me into conversation with them, but I couldn't make heads or tails of what they were talking about."

"Too bad." Jennifer turned her attention back to Pauline. "Do you have anything planned for tomorrow?"

"Naw. Just lay back and let Sunday happen," she replied. "I'll probably sleep until noon. Why, you got something planned?"

"I'd like to spend the day with Mikhail."

"You and me both. Did he ask you?"

"Yes."

"You accepted, didn't you?"

"Not yet."

"Oh my God! For a klutz, you work fast."

"Don't be silly." Jennifer looked up as Mikhail approached her. He immediately took her hand.

"Sorry about that, Jennifer. Lionel is impetuous—and he's always trying to make an impression on someone," Mikhail apologized. "I've got to get back. Just wanted to let you know what was happening."

"Mikhail—about tomorrow—?"

"Yes?"

"Is the invitation still open to go out to your house?"

"By all means."

"Then I accept."

Mikhail stared deeply into her face before he suddenly caught her in his arms and pulled her into a tight embrace. His lips moved to hers and she forgot everything and everyone else. "Don't run away, I'll get back to you—sometime."

"Wow! Oh, wow, Jenni! He kissed you!" Pauline exclaimed.

"Yes, I know."

"I mean *really* kissed you like he meant business."

"Yes, didn't he." Jennifer leaned against the wall to brace herself.

CHAPTER FIVE

The mind and the emotions of an artist often seem to be on a wavelength entirely different from those of the nonartist. Uncontrollable urges to create motivate such persons and force them into somewhat unconventional attitudes and behavioral eccentricities. Jennifer had read many biographies of creative persons, especially those with reputations as celebrated achievers in various fields of the fine arts. Such writings stimulated the desire within her to want to express herself as an artist. Often she had read of bizarre lifestyles and flamboyant habits. She was also aware that many such people had unusual and unconventional sexual appetites—an aspect of their lives which at times they had difficulty accepting or expressing, and which often forced them to lead lives of frustration and/or promiscuity. Such activities were generally only hinted at in the books which she explored, and she had reached the conclusion that she was far too conventional in her way of thinking to really be an outstanding artist. Yet she believed that she could express her talent in such a way that she could be successful in a commercial sense.

On the other hand, that Sunday morning while lying in bed watching autumn sunbeams filter in through the lace curtains of the room assigned to her, Jennifer thought of Mikhail Alexander and his dynamic artistic ability. Long hours of practice and study were reflected in his performance. He certainly was like no one she had ever met—obviously dissimilar to any of the young men she had encountered. She thought of her father, simple, down-to-earth, conservative in many ways. Clarence Logan had what she considered salt-of-the-earth qualities, banal and ordinary in a sense, still uniquely himself in a mundane setting: accomplished in business, financially affluent, a staunch member of the community, with only a few minor bad habits, which he rarely displayed. Perhaps neither of her parents were highly sexually motivated, part of their conservative upbringing and moral indoctrination. She had never thought of her parents in intimate relations, as if it were an aspect of life to which they were completely immune. That, of course, could not be true, since she was noticeably the result of their union. Still, Clarence never uttered a profane word, or anything off-color with a sexual insinuation. Once she heard him say "hell," twice "damn," the effect of which sent her mother into a state of temporary shock. What would their reaction be if they knew that she had romantic thoughts about Mikhail Alexander and that she had become so overwhelmed by his attraction that she speculated what it would be like to make love with him?

Jennifer knew that her father had been raised by a strict-disciplinarian mother who had been divorced by his father, and a domineering grandmother who clung to staunch Victorian attitudes and ethics. Clarence Logan had little chance of growing up like other boys, thus becoming a book-wise outcast among his peers, a fact for which he compensated by developing an adroit business sense. He never smoked or drank for fear of sending his prudent mother and demanding grandmother into a collective tizzy.

Prudence Corkley Logan—the name in itself a dead giveaway—had also emerged from a strict home where an austere approach to religion was dutifully practiced. Both Prudence and her sister Chastity—another dead giveaway—had been raised to believe that sex was a sacred rite, not for pleasure but for the sole purpose of procreation, as had been their parents' apparent attitude and practice. Secretly, both Clarence and Prudence, while strongly imbuing their only offspring with moral and ethical values, wished Jennifer to be less an outcast in contemporary society—but not as promiscuous as other children of her generation. It was with that consideration that they had sent her to Larchmont, which was an easy way out of having to deal with the full-time operation of raising their child and afforded them opportunity to live their own sedate lives without tumultuous interruption.

Jennifer loved and respected her parents and grandparents

because she had been taught to do so. It was easier to conform than to fight a phalanx of highly opinionated and ultraconservative individuals. But Larchmont and Pauline had been instrumental in bringing forth her individuality as well as her talent. Pauline had led her to the discovery of romantic novels as well as into racy contemporary bestsellers and later discussed in vivid detail the romantic and sexual implications involved. The girls helped each other become aware of their bodies, and Jennifer broke away from the mold of family tradition passed to her by persons who appeared to have been born fifty to a hundred years too late.

Caressing her lovely body, especially stimulating the more sensitive places, Jennifer fantasized about Mikhail Alexander and left thoughts of her antecedents behind as problems to deal with at another time.

The day was far too sunny and beautiful to be idled away lying in bed. Having been raised with the "early to bed, early to rise" adage, Jennifer much enjoyed morning hours, especially on Sundays, when most people remained indoors and slept late. She showered and dressed in the same outfit she had worn to the recital and went downstairs, taking her purse and coat with her. No one seemed to be stirring anywhere in the house. After helping herself to a glass of milk and a piece of fruit, and nobody appeared on the scene, she decided to go for a walk.

Autumn aromas and the distant scent of burning leaves were in the air. Squirrels scampered, busy with acorns. Bluejays scolded. In the distance someone was chopping wood. Grass was beginning to turn brown. Chrysanthemums bloomed in profusion and holly berries were becoming plump and red. She plucked a bronze chrysanthemum as she passed a fence where a cascade of flowers were spilling through. She loved the fragrance of natural chrysanthemums, not the practically odorless hothouse varieties. After carrying the blossom for a while, she placed it in a buttonhole as she strolled toward the park where she had been with Mikhail the afternoon before.

Jennifer walked for nearly an hour. Distant church bells ringing caused her to examine her watch. She was in the habit of attending chapel at Larchmont. As she walked toward the corner of Williams and Fourteenth streets, a swirl of rich, multicolored leaves swarmed around her feet and hurriedly sped on past. She decided to visit a church on the corner.

After an hour of inspirational music and a lecture on positive thinking, Jennifer left the church with a wonderful sense of well-being and optimism. Finding her way back to the Watts' house was relatively simple, although she once had to ask directions.

"Where've you been?" Pauline demanded to know as she rushed to greet Jennifer. Dressed in jeans and a mod T-shirt with a collage of musical symbols on it, Pauline appeared disorganized and a little frantic. "Aunt Margarethe and I have searched high and low for you."

"Perhaps not high or low enough," Jennifer quipped. "I awakened early and, not wishing to disturb the household, decided to go for a walk. I ended up attending a charming church and finally wound my way back."

"You gave us a scare," Pauline commented. "You missed not one but three telephone calls. I volunteered to take your place, but he wasn't interested."

"Mikhail?"

"Well, I'm glad to see a little excitement in your face and hear interest in your voice," Pauline said. "I mean, blasé is one thing, but you can carry it to extreme. Had I been expecting a call from Mikhail, believe me I would have been glued to the phone waiting for it."

"He wasn't supposed to call until one." Jennifer removed her coat. "Said he wanted to sleep late."

After enjoying brunch with Pauline and Margarethe, Jennifer had gone to her room to change clothes when Mikhail called again.

"Hi, beautiful! Understand you've been giving your hostesses a bit of a worry." Mikhail sounded robust and happy.

"I went to church."

"Church? Oh yeah, those are the places with steeples and bells," Mikhail kidded. "Sorry. Didn't mean to joke about something that must be important to you. Gorgeous day, isn't it?"

"Nice." Jennifer stood by the window and stared into the yard below. "How soon—?"

"Would you believe fifteen minutes?" Mikhail had a boyish quality to his voice. "Twenty, if you haven't got it together yet."

"Fifteen is fine. How late do we plan to be?"

"Into the wee hours." Mikhail laughed. "Do you have to return at a specific time?"

"Mrs. Watts said she would take us back to school around six," Jennifer replied.

"What time do you actually have to be there?"

"No later than ten."

"I'll take you. Just prepare your things and we'll take them in the car when I pick you up."

"In that case you'd better give me twenty minutes," Jennifer said. "What's planned? I mean, how shall I dress?"

"Casual and comfortable. See you then."

Jennifer stood a moment, gathering her wits before she explained to Pauline and Margarethe how her plans had changed. Pauline helped her pack.

"You certainly work fast once you get started," Pauline observed.

"Maybe Mikhail's the one who progresses passion allegro."

"Huh?"

"You're gaping, Pauline. It's a musical term." Jennifer closed her overnight bag.

Margarethe appeared at the guest-room door. "Why don't we take your things back to Larchmont? You just have the two pieces and it'll be no trouble at all."

"Take the dress bag." Jennifer zipped it. "I don't really know what his plans are, and this skirt and blouse I'm wearing may not be right."

Margarethe laughed. "Jenni, I love Mikhail Alexander dearly. He's a tremendous artist. Just be careful he doesn't seduce you with that magnetic charm of his."

"Did you say 'seduce,' Aunt Mar?" Pauline asked. "Oh God!"

"Nothing to panic about." Margarethe laughed. "I'm certain he's no different from any other boy or man you may go out with. I'm only warning because I know neither of you are terribly experienced when it comes to dating. I don't want you to be swept away by his overwhelming personality. Be careful, that's all—and enjoy yourself."

"How's she going to enjoy herself if she has to be so darned careful?" Pauline asked. "If it were me, I'd throw caution to the wind and get down to essentials."

"Really, Pauline!" Jennifer scolded. "What girls in novels do, and what happens in real life, are two different things. I'll manage myself with Mikhail."

"I'm certain you will, Jenni," Margarethe encouraged.

"Thanks for a wonderful weekend." Jennifer started for the door. "My coat's downstairs."

"I enjoyed having you. And I must say, you certainly charmed my friends. We will do it again." Margarethe let Pauline go ahead of her.

"Need any last-minute advice?" Pauline asked as Mikhail's sports car pulled into the drive.

"None from you, thanks." Jennifer laughed and thanked them again for the weekend. Moments later she stepped outside to meet him.

Mikhail wore a pair of brief walking shorts and a knit shirt. "I may be stretching the season, but I love to wear this sort of thing. Just one bag?"

"Mrs. Watts is taking my dress bag back."

Mikhail held the door for her, closed it and waved to Margarethe as Pauline arrived at the door, Polaroid in hand, and snapped a hurried shot of the handsome pianist.

Mikhail chuckled as he slid onto the bucket seat. He turned with a smile to Jennifer. "Comfortable?"

"Trying to be."

Mikhail put his hand to her knee and patted it. "Have no fear, my beauty, you're in safe hands." He wheeled the car out the driveway and onto the road. "Purrs like a kitten, doesn't she? My dad may be a lot of bark and growl, but he's generous. Not that he has to buy my love—I love him anyway. He's always dragged his feet when it came to me playing the piano, but one of his friends once told me he brags up a storm about me when I'm not around to hear." He glanced over at Jennifer. "Hey, I was just kidding this morning when I said that about church. I don't go regularly, but I go. And not only when I'm playing special music for a service."

"I thought you might have been joking," Jennifer remarked

with a wide smile. "I believe autumn and spring are my favorite times of the year—and I'm not certain which I like best."

"I like something special about all seasons," Mikhail said as he headed the car west toward Golden. "Thought we'd just drive around for a while before we head for my place."

"Your place?"

"Anxiety?"

Jennifer tried to laugh. "Not really. I'd love to see where you live. Philip Franklin was telling me about it the night of the recital."

"I wouldn't be surprised if he dropped by sometime this afternoon." Mikhail adjusted his position. "He's as diligent about his dancing as I am with the piano. Guess he told you he was doing a program the week after next. If you'd like, I'll take you to see it. I wouldn't miss it."

Nearly an hour later Mikhail turned the car off the main road and drove a mile and a half through an isolated area, brown fields with the remnants of harvest. The road curved through gigantic glacier-upturned slabs of red rock.

Jennifer caught her first glimpse of the modern structure positioned at the crest of a flat-topped hill resembling a mesa. It had been created to fit into the rugged surrounding countryside. A wall of nearly solid glass windows reflected the sun, making the building glow golden.

"That's Largo," Mikhail pointed.

"Largo?"

"My house. My maternal grandfather conceived and built it. He was quite an architect and contractor in his day. Many of the modern buildings in Denver and the surrounding area were his creations." Mikhail spoke with pride. "After his death my grandmother maintained it for a few years, but it wasn't the same without him. When she decided to take a small place in the city, she gave it to me as a gift. I'm her only grandchild. She said my grandfather dreamed it up when he first heard me play at eleven. He called it Largo because that was a particular movement I played that fascinated him."

"Yours? What a wonderful gift!"

"My grandfather always wanted me to have it," Mikhail continued. "He set up an endowment fund for its perpetuation. I love it. Sometimes when I'm deep in concentration at the piano, I can sense my grandfather's presence. Hey, don't get spooked out. There's no ghost prowling around the place. I guess I just think about him and the way he loved to hear me play. He offered to pay for my lessons. My dad always said Granddad shamed him into sponsoring my studies. Sometimes Grandma comes out and stays with me to see that I eat properly."

"You're fortunate to have such support from your family," Jennifer said as the car pulled up the final incline to the top. "What a glorious view from here!"

"I like it. Wait until night. I'm far enough away from city lights that the stars are overwhelming." Mikhail steered the car around the last bend and pulled into the large, well-manicured parking area.

Many of the shrubs around the house had been wrapped with burlap for the winter. The stately firs stood as sentinels along with other hardy plants.

"Who would believe there'd be such wonderful trees here?" Jennifer asked.

Mikhail caught her hand as they walked toward the front door. He stopped, looked down into her face before he turned her around to see the view.

"What a spectacle!" Jennifer exclaimed.

Mikhail stood behind her, his hands on her shoulders. "This is my kingly domain. Now all I need is to find a queen to reign with me."

"Lucky queen, whoever she turns out to be," Jennifer sighed. "This is absolutely breathtaking."

"I'm glad you like it." Mikhail wrapped his arms about her and kissed the top of her head. "I like the feel of you." A moment later he disconnected his hold and unlocked the door. "There's a great place for afternoon sun on the other side. I'll show you around first."

The house was built on three levels, with solar heating, glass roofs in places and almost magical indirect lighting from the sun's rays. The entire design had a modern ambience. The rooms were large, with few pieces of furniture. A white concert grand piano dominated the salon. Mikhail snapped on a switch and stereo music seemed to come from all directions.

Jennifer was still gasping at the beauty of the main room when Mikhail pulled her toward the spacious kitchen and the equally large dining room with a fabulous view of Denver in the distance. Three sides were practically solid glass.

"I'd hate to have to wash the windows," Jennifer remarked.

Mikhail laughed. "I have men who come in twice a month and wash them all. The entire maintenance is jobbed in. Granddad arranged for it years ago."

"What happens in the winter during heavy snows?"

"I live mostly in the den, bedroom and kitchen then," he explained, "if I'm here. Sometimes I like being snowed in. I've plenty of supplies. It's neat."

"Must get lonely."

"I never feel lonely when I have my music." He pulled her toward the den, which had a sunken floor, steps leading down into it. Around the square were upholstered platform seats. The center of the square was a round-hooded fireplace. On the upper level was a smaller grand piano, a wall of books, a desk and cabinets. "I do most of my work here—all of my composing." Two sides of the room were windows.

Finally, Mikhail led her to the top floor, which had three bedrooms and a large artist's studio. "Granddad did much of his work here. I use it when I get the urge to paint—usually watercolors. It's sunny and bright."

"I love it," Jennifer uttered, still bedazzled by the overall impression. "You're to be envied."

Again Mikhail stared down into her face. "Did you happen to bring a bathing suit along?"

"Don't tell me you have a swimming pool, too?"

"In the basement. My grandparents both enjoyed swimming."

"Swimming didn't even enter my mind when I planned for the weekend," Jennifer admitted.

"I was thinking more in terms of catching some of the sun's rays," Mikhail said. "No big thing. I've something that will fit you. Come into the bedroom. We'll catch the pool and the basement studio later."

Jennifer tried not to lag behind, but Mikhail could tell she was hesitant. He let go of her hand when he went to a bureau and came up with two pieces of a bikini bathing suit.

"It's adjustable."

"Who does it belong to?" Jennifer asked as she skeptically looked at the skimpy outfit.

"Would you believe my grandmother?" Mikhail laughed at her incredulous expression. "She only wore it once. She decided pale blue wasn't her color, so she abandoned it. There's a bathroom, go change."

Jennifer had worn what she called abbreviated swim attire, but never anything quite as brief as that. Still, she thought, if it was good enough for Granny, why not?

Mikhail appeared in an equally diminutive bathing suit, revealing a sensuously attractive body, well-tanned and nicely proportioned for his height. He carried two beach towels.

"Hey, I like," Mikhail exclaimed as he surveyed Jennifer.

"Don't ogle—I'll blush," Jennifer protested.

"You don't want me to admire your body?" he teased. "I've a couple of Band Aids you can apply if it will help your modesty." He stepped to her, looked down into her face and lowered his head to kiss her. Those magnificent hands touched her bare skin, gently over her shoulders and arms. "Yes, I like very much." He took her hand and pulled her through sliding doors onto a terrace outside the bedroom.

After spreading the towels on side-by-side chaise lounges, he motioned for her to sit.

"Need some tanning lotion?" he asked. "I'll be more than happy to apply it for you."

"No—no, I'll be fine without it," Jennifer stammered.

"Okay. We've only got about forty-five minutes of good sun before a breeze comes up," Mikhail said as he positioned himself on one of the towels.

Jennifer hesitantly sat on the other and leaned back in a semi-sitting posture.

"You've never had a man make love to you before, have you?" Mikhail asked a few minutes later.

"How can you—? I mean, what makes you think so?"

"You're too uptight." Mikhail held his face upward toward the sun.

"I've always dreamed of knowing a girl who was inexperienced," Mikhail said. "Totally. So many I've met have been playing around since they were in their teens, hopping from one guy to another. They're too eager and have lovemaking down to a routine. Maybe I'm old-fashioned in ways."

"What makes you say that?"

"I've had my share of fun and games," Mikhail admitted. "I find it fascinating only to a point. So you go with a girl for a while, you do everything, and when you don't come up with something new, interest begins to dwindle. I'm an artist, my real lover is the piano, and I daily make love to it for long hours at a time. Someday I'll find a girl who will fall in love with me and will mean as much to me as the piano does. Sounds funny, doesn't it? Didn't mean it to. It's just that I feel when the right girl comes along, she'll be as much a part of me as my music is."

"I think I understand what you're saying." Jennifer tried not to sound confused. "You need someone who is as artistically inclined as you are, in a sense, one who understands what it's like to be creative."

"Precisely." He opened his eyes and caught her gazing at him. "You understand. I try to explain that to some girls and they look at me like I had three ears. I never pretended to be like other guys, the football jocks or the routine mechanics. The fact is, I don't like to think of myself as being like other pianists or creative artists, but as uniquely me. If I desired to be ordinary, I could never excel as a concert pianist, or as a composer. Once I did some architectural renderings in watercolor for my grandfather. He took one look and said they were gorgeous, magnificently inventive—but they would never work for the purpose he needed, which required exactness of line and proportion. I went back to the easel and ultimately came up with what he wanted. When he asked if I enjoyed making the second set, I told him it was like doing a coloring book and, quite frankly, it bored me silly. He threw his arms around me—Granddad was always extremely affectionate—and explained that I had a special talent, an artistic gift, and I would be foolish to ever try to be like anyone else. I've always remembered that."

"I don't know about such things," Jennifer commented, "but

I would guess that what he said was true. He must have died quite young."

"On the contrary. Granddad was well into his thirties before he married," Mikhail related. "He was in his mid-sixties before I was born, although in appearance he looked twenty-five to thirty years younger. He never struck me as an old man until the last six months of his life. He said the only regret he had about waiting so long to marry was that he could not spend more time with me. Never having had a son of his own, I was the boy he had always wanted. My father often became jealous of my relationship with Granddad."

"If you were that close to him," Jennifer said as her eyes swept over Mikhail's body again, "it wouldn't surprise me if his spirit were still around you much of the time."

"I believe it is." Mikhail sat on the chaise beside her. "Most girls think I'm weird when I talk about Granddad like this. They even suspect that Largo is haunted. But it's not a bad haunting, quite the opposite." He outlined her face with his fingers. "I want to make love to you, Jennifer."

She tensed.

"Not now, not this minute, but sometime." He put his face to hers and kissed lightly. "I want you to fall in love with me, not with just a silly infatuation that women get when they hear me play, but to fall deeply in love. It won't happen after one kiss or a Sunday afternoon at Largo. I've seen you in my mind's eye, in my dreams, so when I actually saw you in person, I knew I had at last found you." He stared into her eyes with such a magical quality that she could only respond by bringing her face forward for him to kiss again.

As his turgid lips touched hers and his liquid tongue forced them apart, Jennifer reacted to the electrical impact flowing through her. Her hands wrapped around his body, locked in position at first until they began to explore curiously. What she felt flooded her with a greater sense of excitement, liquid heat exhilarating her to ecstatic desire.

Mikhail kissed over her face and down her neck, about her shoulders and onto her chest. He knew she wanted as much as he did at that moment, and it would have been so easy to have his way with her. But he was an artist who knew well how to manipulate his audience and bring them to a thunderous response, not with only one glorious passage. The entire composition was the masterpiece, and it took time to progress from the initial chord to the final triumphant climax.

"Mikhail—you were right about me," Jennifer moaned as his face again pressed against hers. "There were times when I might have submitted, but I couldn't. I had never been with you."

"And you will not completely submit to me now," Mikhail said judiciously. "This is just the opening prelude, the initial establishing of the motif. We're a long way from passion allegro."

"How far?"

"When I make up my mind to go after something," he replied, "I usually accomplish it. I must think of you as an elaborate sonata and I'm only now going through the finger exercises of getting into it. There are pages and pages of notes, chords, arpeggios and variations ahead of us. When we reach the ultimate climax, I want you to be so thoroughly mine that by the time we begin the grand concerto, we will explore it unequivocably as one. I expect many fantasies, impromptus, concerti, sonatas and what have you. I want you to become my instrument of artistic pleasure." Again his mouth slid to hers. His hand explored her body, touching, stimulating, exciting, before he gently eased her into less exotic sensation. He held her close, their heads and much of their bodies pressed tightly together.

A breeze came up and rustled the beach towels.

"We'd better go inside," Mikhail finally said.

"Prelude over?"

"Oh no, just beginning," he assured her. "Only this portion of it must end." He gathered the towels. "It would probably be well if you took a nice warm shower before you dress."

Jennifer was slightly alarmed at what seemed to be a sudden change of attitude. Although he led her by the hand into the house, she perceived that he had become remote.

CHAPTER SIX

When Jennifer emerged after a leisurely shower, during which time romantic speculations about Mikhail soared wildly, she heard the sound of the piano coming from another part of the house. She dressed and made certain her appearance was precisely right before she wandered downstairs toward the sound.

Still clad in the diminutive bikini, which was almost obscured by his position on the piano stool, Mikhail was playing a Chopin variation with splashy runs up and down the keyboard. Had she had a sketchpad, she would have drawn him as he performed at the white concert grand.

Mikhail was lost in deep contemplation as his fingers danced with remarkable ease and skill. His body and emotions writhed with the music as if it was a total part of him.

Jennifer remained across the room, admiring the spectacle. Her fantasies were stimulated. Yet she wondered if he were not taking out sexual frustration on the piano. Why did she think that?

A hand touched her shoulder and she reacted with a squeak of surprise, certain if she were to turn around she would behold the ghost of Mikhail's maternal grandfather. Instead, as she perceived the firmness of the hand with a definite physical sensation, she glanced around to see the familiar countenance of Philip Franklin.

"Didn't mean to startle you," Philip said.

"I had no idea you were here."

"I know. Just arrived before Mikhail started to play," Philip replied. "I was in the kitchen checking the roast for him."

Jennifer faced him and saw that he was also wearing a brief outfit, similar to the posing strap he had worn in her life-drawing class.

"Dinner won't be for an hour," Philip announced. "I'm going downstairs to practice for awhile."

"Dressed like that?" Jennifer gasped.

"I would be wearing less if I hadn't been told that you were here." He laughed. His attention turned from her questioning eyes to Mikhail. "Magnificent, isn't he? He may go on like that for an hour or more. He's in a trance—self-induced. I should imagine he's romping in Elysian fields or experiencing something like a psychedelic vision of eternal mysteries. That's the way he is when he plays. The notes become second nature to him, they simply come out; but the emotion and the fury are the outgrowth of what he is sensing in the innermost part of him."

"You sound as if you know him well."

"In a way, I do." Philip smiled. "When I dance—or even when I pose like I did for you—I put myself into a similar trance. Mikhail taught me how. My body experiences one thing while my fantasies expand far beyond. You may come down and watch me work out if you like, or remain here and watch the genius. I imagine you'll choose the latter. In any case, tell him that the roast will be done in an hour—if he stops playing by then."

Jennifer watched Philip depart before she found a chair on the side of the room and diligently observed as Mikhail continued to play.

She was somewhat perplexed by the situation. Never had she seen such a display of control and magnitude. There was no doubt in her mind that he was a unique individual, one of a kind. Still observing him and the tremendous masculinity he exuded, her own fantasies began to wander and romantic speculation increased.

When the final chords were sounded, Mikhail's rigid body fell limp as he slumped over the keyboard. He remained in that position for several moments while he appeared to bring himself out of the trance. Finally, he raised his head, glanced over at Jennifer and smiled. He approached her with long-legged strides and slid onto a couch near where she was seated. He held out his hand and she went to him.

"That was inspirational," Jennifer exclaimed.

"You were my inspiration." He pulled her to him. "I'm sorry

I suggested you change. That was merely my first climax. Now I am ready to make love to you." His mouth pressed heavily over hers.

"Mikhail—" she said when his mouth freed hers and began to move over other parts of her, "I have to ask you to respect the fact that I've been raised with old-fashioned moral values."

"Outside you were willing."

"I responded without thinking," Jennifer replied.

Mikhail suddenly stood and pushed her aside. He went toward the piano and leaned against it. Jennifer was quickly on her feet and stood behind him.

"I'm sorry." She put her hand on his shoulder and let it run down his arm. "I want you—you know I do. But you said something about falling in love."

Mikhail slowly turned to her. "No, I'm sorry. I apologize for coming on to you so fast." He looked from one of her eyes to the other, studying them. A smile began to melt his intense expression. "I lost myself in the music—which I quite often do. My concept of time was temporarily off." He put his hands to her arms. "I want you, Jenni, I want you with all my heart and soul. I may have been a stranger to you when we met, but I've seen you, known you, loved you in my projected vision. You are the one person I wish to worship and adore. And at this moment I am so overwhelmed with desire—" His lips again touched hers, his tongue thrust and he clasped her to him with such strength that she thought he would surely crush her. As his enthusiasm mounted and she was again propelled with liquid excitement, he released his hold and dashed back to the piano stool. His hands pounced with a thundering display of fury.

Jennifer remained where he left her as the music seemed to vibrate through every particle of her. Tears came. Hand over hand she moved down the piano until she could see the violence of his fingers over the keys. Then she slowly inched toward him until she placed her hands on his naked shoulders and gently eased her body against his. She remained in that position until he finished playing.

Mikhail turned his head to kiss her. "I was making love to you, then. Now I think I should swim for ten minutes before I prepare dinner."

"Can I help?"

"You can join me in the pool. You don't need a suit. I swim without one." He stood and embraced her again. "No. Let's work on the first layer of that cake—we'll get to the cherry at another time." He peeled himself from her, retaining only a light grip about her hand. "One thing a pianist learns is ultimate control. Why don't you just explore around for a few minutes? I won't be long."

Never had Jennifer gone through so many physical and emotional changes in such a relatively short period of time. Her head was still awhirl and her body tingled with residual sensation. She could imagine what Pauline Maples would have done in such a situation. Although she was fond of Pauline, she had long since learned that they were two very different people.

She strolled outside and watched the long afternoon shadows form, making grotesque images as the sun eased lower behind the upturned red rocks. Occasionally, she heard a bird's call. The tumult and shouting within had begun to calm and a quiet sense of serenity flowed through her. She considered things that Mikhail had said and wondered if he were in some way testing her, making certain she was not like those other girls he had known who "hopped from one man to another." Certainly with such stimulation, she could see how a person could become that way—throwing caution to the wind, as Pauline would say.

"Hi," Philip interrupted her thoughts. He had pulled into a snugly fitting pair of jeans and a T-shirt. "I often enjoy watching the shadows increase. It's much nicer in the summer. The breeze can get chilly."

"Do you come here often?" Jennifer asked.

"As often as possible. Many weekends I stay over. One of the guest rooms has been assigned to me," Philip explained. "Mikhail is busy preparing dinner. He suggested that I might show you the basement studio where I work out—and the swimming pool."

"Fine."

Philip led her downstairs to the enormously large room known as the studio. Track lighting throughout, with dimmer switches, made it possible to light specific areas.

"Mikhail has performed a few concerts for his friends in the salon on the main floor," Philip related. "And I've given some dance recitals down here—again only to a select few. Sometimes Mikhail works out with me." He laughed. "Don't get me wrong, he doesn't aspire to be a dancer, too, but he likes the exercise, and he can be helpful when I'm trying to work out pieces of choreography I can't handle by myself. My dream is to someday choreograph a ballet to his music. I'm afraid that's many moons away. Come and see the swimming pool."

They passed through a hallway and into the pool area. It was quite large, with a glass top at the far end.

"Absolutely amazing," Jennifer exclaimed as she stared at the enormous pool.

"Mikhail's a fantastic swimmer," Philip said. "I'm not bad, but I'm no competition to him. Great exercise."

"I swim a little myself," Jennifer admitted. "Just for my own amusement. Do you both swim without suits?"

"Always," Philip replied lightly. "At least when I'm alone or it's just the two of us. I can't speak for Mikhail when I'm not here."

After a candlelight dinner, Philip excused himself to adjourn to the basement again.

"I'll light a fire in the den," Mikhail suggested. "We can sit in there."

Twenty minutes later Jennifer dreamily stared into the fire while Mikhail sat at the piano and serenaded her. Many questions came to mind that someday she might dare to ask.

"I suppose I should be excited," Mikhail said a while later after he turned on the stereo and joined Jennifer on the hip-consuming cushions around the fire.

"About what?"

"Cleo Dennison. I've signed with her to be my manager," Mikhail related. "I believe I'm ready for professional exposure as a concert pianist. I don't really expect to be an overnight sensation, but it's time I let the critics have a crack at me."

"I'm certain if you perform anything like you did the other night, that you'll have the critics eating out of your hand."

"That could be messy." Mikhail laughed.

"You know what I mean." Jennifer curled up to him.

"Yes, I know. Guess I have a weird sense of humor," Mikhail

said before he kissed the back of her hand. "I like this—being with you." He gazed into the flames for a few moments. "You know, I'm grateful to you."

"For what?"

"Giving me perspective—and maybe taking me off the hook." Again he kissed her hand.

"Explain."

"Usually when I'm in a close situation with a girl, she expects me to perform—and I don't mean on the piano," Mikhail explained. "Sure, we talk and sit around a little, but always I have the feeling that they're with me for one reason. Maybe it's my imagination. But your 'old-fashioned moral values' set me at ease. I realized I could be me and just relax and have fun getting to know you. That wasn't my initial reaction. But after an invigorating swim, I reached the conclusion that it was good. If two people spend much time together, it can't always be in bed. I guess my ideas have become somewhat perverted by the fact that girls rush at me, turned on when they hear me play. Admittedly, I've taken advantage of the situation from time to time. Generally, after the cymbals crash and the kettle drums cease rumbling, I discover we don't have much to talk about—and little of mutual interest. Sound funny? Maybe."

"Not at all," Jennifer replied. "I saw how the women reacted to you at the concert, and how they swarmed over you at the reception. I thought to myself it must be difficult for you. Personally, I'm happy quietly doing my artwork, drawing, painting, whatever. I become very absorbed in it. Pauline Maples can't understand how I can be so content. But I think she has her mind on men twenty-four hours a day."

"Have you ever been in love, Jenni?"

Jennifer thought a few moments. "I've had crushes on a couple of men teachers, but I'd hardly call that being in love. Why do you ask?"

"Just curious."

"Have you?"

"I don't think so. I've liked a few people—you know, for the physical thing," Mikhail stated, "but I don't think I've ever really been in love. I came to the conclusion that you can't equate sexual satisfaction with love. Okay, it's better if you really like someone—but really being devoted to one person and absolutely in love—I don't know about that. I wish I did. I believe it would help me in many aspects of my life, including my music. There was a girl in high school I had a tremendous crush on. She only liked burly football players. I guess, because I couldn't have her, I wanted her all the more. She married a football hero once they graduated from school. He blamed her because he couldn't use a college scholarship he'd been offered, since he had to earn a living to support her and the kid they had right away. Two kids later and he left her. By then he'd become a slob and she wasn't much better. I thought after that, gee, I was lucky I didn't play football."

Jennifer laughed. "I'm glad you didn't."

"Why?"

"I'd hate to think of you giving up your piano."

"No woman could have made me do that." Mikhail examined his watch. "I don't mean to rush you, and God knows, I love you being here, but I don't want you to be late getting back."

"That's thoughtful of you." She kissed his hand.

"Soon you'll have to show me some of your drawings."

"I'd like to."

Mikhail kissed her warmly before he stood and pulled her to her feet. "Why don't you just wait here for a few minutes and I'll dash down and tell Philip we're leaving. He can tend to the fire."

Jennifer ran her fingers over the piano keys in the den, picked out a simple melody she had learned as a child and tried to keep her thoughts light about Mikhail.

When Mikhail returned to the den, he was wearing a sheepskin coat. "I started the car so the heater would warm it inside. Once the sun goes down up here, it gets very cold." He handed her her coat.

"Thank you."

He helped her into the coat, then wrapped his arms around her. "You've been most considerate coming to visit today—and understanding."

"My pleasure."

"I wish you weren't going—but I'm glad you are."

"Why such a contradiction?" Jennifer asked as they walked toward the front door.

"Because I want to really want you," Mikhail said. "I want the mystery to last until the desire in each of us reaches colossal heights."

It seemed a million stars twinkled in the clear night sky as they hurried toward the car. Mikhail held the door for her.

"Why do you wish the desire to reach colossal heights?" Jennifer asked as the car began to move down the incline.

"Because I already like you very much," he replied. He reached for her hand. "I expect even stronger feelings will be generated as we get to know each other better."

"I hope so." Jennifer squeezed his hand and he squeezed back.

During the return ride, Mikhail spoke of his family, again of his grandfather in endearing terms. Jennifer told of her family and the staid background from which she came. She even related tales about Larchmont and Pauline Maples.

Mikhail laughed at some of the things she said, and related sympathetically to others. The time hurried by fast, and before they knew it, they had arrived in Boulder and ultimately at Larchmont. The darkly shadowed buildings presented a cold, imposing sight.

"I'll help you in with your bag," Mikhail offered.

"It's light. I can manage," Jennifer replied, thinking that she did not want to arouse suspicious opinions from anyone at Larchmont.

Mikhail turned off the engine and put his arm around her. "I'm impressed, Jenni, I really am."

"I had a wonderful time."

Mikhail's mouth was again atop hers. She responded at first, then became worried and softly pushed him away.

"I don't want anyone to see us," Jennifer whispered. "Please understand."

"I do." He nibbled kisses over her face. "Maybe next weekend we can do something again."

"I hope so. But if I get caught out here, I could get grounded," Jennifer protested.

"But you've graduated, you're nineteen, an adult."

"I know. But as long as I remain here, I have to adhere to

their rules," Jennifer explained. "And according to my watch, I have exactly a minute and a half to get inside."

"One thirty-second kiss and I'll let you go." Again he overwhelmed her with his sensational mouth, the exploring of his hands, just the aura of his being.

Jennifer ran, bag in hand, to the front door. She turned and waved before entering.

"Oh Lord, Jenni, you just made it by the skin of your teeth," Pauline exclaimed when Jennifer pushed into the room they shared. "I did my best to cover for you. You know how snoopy certain people can be. And speaking of snoopy, tell me everything that happened. I'm dying with fever blisters to know."

"I'll tell you later. I really don't want to talk about it now."

"That bad?" Pauline asked as she landed on the bed.

"Not bad."

"That good?" Pauline persisted.

Jennifer yawned and stretched before she began putting her clothing away. "It was adequate."

"Jennifer!"

When Mikhail arrived back at Largo, Philip greeted him with the information that Cleo Dennison had called him from New York.

"Thanks, buddy."

Philip watched him for a moment. "Do you like her?"

"Who? Cleo Dennison?"

"No. Jennifer Logan."

Mikhail winked. "Yeah, I think I like her very much."

Philip swallowed comment and watched as Mikhail went to phone.

CHAPTER SEVEN

The next three days Jennifer acted as if she were waltzing on air, her mind in the clouds. She tried not to think constantly of Mikhail, but that was close to impossible. She attempted to act normal and appear to have her feet on the ground, but every so often she gave the impression that she was slowly wafting upward.

"Jenni, has someone been tampering with your marbles?" Pauline asked on Wednesday when they met to go to lunch in the dining hall.

"I don't play with marbles," Jennifer returned dreamily.

"Yeah. And it looks like you're not playing with a full deck either. And that silly grin. People are beginning to think you're taking some kind of loony pills or something," Pauline continued. "I could have laughed at some of the comments I've heard about you."

"So people talk, so what?" Jennifer passed the matter off lightly. "I really haven't much of an appetite."

"Maybe you should see the doctor."

"I'm perfectly all right, Pauline."

"Uh-huh." Pauline studied her friend. "Maybe you've stayed too long at Larchmont. After all, you've graduated."

"Perhaps I feel secure here," Jennifer said. "Being at Larchmont is a little stifling, but if I were with my parents, I'd be absolutely suffocated."

"Your drawings are terrific," Pauline encouraged. "Why don't you try to sell them, or find a job illustrating for a magazine or a book or something?"

"Easier said than done. I doubt I'd locate many avenues to sell in Denver."

"Then go to Chicago, or New York, or where?—Los Angeles," Pauline stated, "anywhere."

"Maybe I will—someday." That dreamy look returned to Jennifer's eyes.

After lunch the girls stopped by the dormitory to check for mail. Jennifer received a letter from her grandmother and one from Mikhail Alexander.

In his letter Mikhail professed his love for her and his desire to make love to her. He had been thinking about their situation and how he had been so impressed with her beauty and charm, and how he had thought of little else but her. His words went on for a page and a half. Once the principal theme was stated, he embellished upon it and concluded with the thought that he believed that she was the one girl in the entire world with whom he could fall deeply in love.

Jennifer's mind became even more clouded with romantic notions. Mikhail was vivid in her imagination.

Thursday evening, while ensconced in her room at the drawing table, Jennifer was informed that a young man was in the main hall waiting to see her. Her heart fluttered as she quickly changed into a simple dress and sweater, brushed her hair and applied makeup. She tried not to run from the dormitory, but it was difficult to keep a ladylike pace.

Her balloon of anticipation deflated when, instead of finding Mikhail waiting, she discovered Philip Franklin.

"Hi, Jenni," Philip said as he crossed to her. He was neatly dressed in a sportcoat and tie, slacks and loafers. His handsome appearance had attracted the attention of several girls.

Jennifer conquered her disappointment. "It's good to see you, Philip. What brings you to Larchmont?"

"I thought perhaps we could have a little talk," he replied.

"Okay. I'm certain we can find a quiet place in the social hall," Jennifer said and directed the way.

Philip felt somewhat awkward going toward the social hall, especially when he encountered several girls who had been in the life-drawing class for which he had posed. "Maybe they won't recognize me with my clothes on."

"What do you want to talk about?" Jennifer asked once they were comfortably situated.

"You." Philip appeared temporarily tongue-tied. "Well, actually about you and Mikhail."

"What about us?"

"I love Mikhail like a brother and I'm very fond of you," Philip stated. "Mikhail has told me about his feeling for you. He realizes that they've developed unusually fast and he believes your feelings for him are similar."

"Is there something wrong with that?"

"I wished I smoked," Philip confessed. "It would give me something to do with my hands and maybe make me less nervous."

"Nervous? About what?"

"Jenni—Mikhail is a tremendous creative talent," Philip said. "He's a magnificent concert pianist and his compositions are by far superior to most works being written today. He's a genius."

"I could almost tell."

"Artistic, creative geniuses are not like other people."

"I should think they wouldn't be," Jennifer returned, uncertain how to react to the situation.

"Living with a genius can be extremely difficult," he stated. "I have a cousin who's married to one—and her life is a perfect hell most of the time."

"Why?"

"Because her husband's off in his own creative world three quarters or more of the time. He's so absorbed in what he is creating that he loses conception of everything but his work. He's away a lot, traveling. My cousin believes he simply takes her for granted. She waits endless hours for him to return home, and even when he's there, he's preoccupied, so she continues to wait in anticipation until he finally remembers her and takes a few minutes away to express his love. Often he's mentally and physically exhausted when that happens. She ends up with a minute part of him, and enormous frustration."

"Why are you telling me this?" Jennifer asked.

"I think you should know what it's like to be involved with a creative genius."

Jennifer considered his statement. "Does your cousin work?"

"No. She just keeps house for him and raises their two children. It occupies her time and she's constantly busy, but it certainly wasn't the life she idealized when she agreed to marry him." Philip reached for her hand. "I want you to be aware of what you might be getting into with Mikhail."

"I appreciate your concern," Jennifer said as she looked down at his hand holding hers. "The difference in your cousin and me is that I have my artwork. I spend many, many wonderful hours in solitude drawing. Once I can begin earning money from it, I'll become preoccupied with my creativity, too."

"Just be careful, Jenni. Weigh the circumstances and the consequences. Don't rush in with your heart when your eyes are closed."

Jennifer asked if he had ulterior motives for speaking to her as he had done.

"No. I'm a creative person, too. Perhaps not a genius such as Mikhail is, but I like to believe I have talent." Philip smiled reassuringly at her. "I spend long hours dancing, thinking up choreography. I rarely have time for anything else. But I'm content doing what I do. Maybe someday I'll discover a physical-romantic side of myself that I wish to explore, but right now my love is my dancing. What ulterior motives could I have other than to want you to be aware of aspects of a situation you may not have considered?"

"Thank you. I'll take to heart what you've said. I suppose it would be much simpler to fall in love with an auto mechanic or a shopkeeper or someone with a mundane and ordinary life. I could always tend babies and do the laundry and have my drawing on the side." Jennifer frowned. "But I think I'd go plain nuts with an ordinary man—especially after I've known Mikhail Alexander. I'll probably have to do a lot of adjusting in my thinking as well as in other aspects of my life, but I'll manage with determination."

"I'm sure that you can," Philip returned. "Remember, I'm your friend. Please call on me anytime you need to talk."

An hour after Philip left, Jennifer received a telephone call from Mikhail, asking if he could meet her at five the next night.

"For the evening?" Jennifer asked.

"I was hoping for the entire weekend."

"I'm not supposed to be away from Larchmont that long unless a responsible adult guarantees my safety," Jennifer said.

"I'm a responsible adult."

"Responsible *older* adult."

"I'll call Margarethe Watts and have her tell a little white lie," said Mikhail.

"Maybe it would be better just for the evening."

"No. I want you for the entire weekend."

Jennifer considered his statement. "Okay, call Mrs. Watts and see if she'll do it."

"I intend to get you out of Larchmont once and for all," Mikhail stated.

"How do you expect to do that?"

"I may have to marry you," Mikhail affirmed.

"Just so I'll leave Larchmont?"

"No, Jenni," his voice softened, "no, because I think I'm falling in love with you—I mean deeply in love with you. Darn!"

"What's wrong?"

"I hadn't meant to say that over the phone," Mikhail explained. "I had been thinking more in terms of soft candlelight, romantic music and maybe sparkling wine. That's not a proposal, mind you, but it's damned close to one."

Jennifer tried to laugh away the trembling excitement within her. Impossible!

"Are you laughing at me?" Mikhail questioned.

"No, no, dearest Mikhail, not at all," Jennifer replied. "I believe that I am developing extremely strong love feelings for you, too. As Pauline would say, to hell with Larchmont if it stands in the way of what I really want."

"When did Pauline say that?"

"A number of times. It isn't important." Jennifer tossed her head back with determination. "Don't bother to call Mrs. Watts. I'll speak to the headmistress myself, explain that I'm an adult and I don't wish to be treated as an underaged minor any longer."

"That's my girl!"

Surprisingly, Jennifer encountered no difficulty with the headmistress, who only warned her with words of wisdom to be careful.

"You're going to spend the entire weekend with him?" Pauline questioned later that night as she bounced onto Jennifer's bed. "Oh my God!"

"Don't crinkle or raise your eyebrows at me, Pauline Maples," Jennifer scolded. "I told you there were three bedrooms in his house. Philip has his, Mikhail has his, and I'll probably stay in the third."

"Oh, come on, Jenni! Grow up! Why mess up an extra bed?" Pauline sat on the edge of the bed beside Jennifer and put her arm around her shoulder. "Hey, look, I'll give you some of my pills."

"Why do you have pills?"

"Just in case. Who knows? I might get lucky." Pauline laughed. "That's not the point. I'd be willing with an absolute stranger, but it's different with you. The guy's practically in love with you. This is an age of enlightenment, not the Dark Ages."

Mikhail was waiting at the gate to pick up Jennifer precisely at five. He put her suitcase and dress bag in the trunk after holding the door for her. A few moments later he scooted onto the seat behind the wheel.

"What's on the agenda for tonight?" Jennifer asked as he started the engine.

"First, I'm going to pull up the road to where there's a grove of trees, park in the shadows, and kiss you silly," Mikhail warned. "Then I'm going to take you to a fabulous restaurant for dinner, after which we'll attend a concert. One of Lionel Adams' former students is playing with the Denver Symphony. There'll be a little party afterward. Ultimately, we'll drive out to Largo."

"In a state of sheer exhaustion," Jennifer inserted.

"If so, we'll get a good night's sleep and let tomorrow bring what it will." Mikhail did not turn off the motor when he parked beneath the trees. In a moment he had Jennifer in his embrace, kissing her even more passionately—if that is possible—than he had done before. She responded and kissed back without hesitation or qualms.

"Mikhail—" she gasped when she came up for air.

"Fantastic! You're improving! Maybe I am, too." He kissed

her again. "I do love you, Jenni, I do. You've been on my mind all week. I even wrote a little piece which I simply call 'Jennifer.' I can't wait to play it for you." He kissed her again. "You can't know how I've missed you, how I've wanted to drop everything and drive to Larchmont to snatch you away from whatever was holding you here." His lips again found hers. "I had a coaching session with Lionel Adams this afternoon. He noticed a difference in both me and my playing. Being in love seems to show in everything I do."

"Are you certain you're in love?" Jennifer asked, her lips touching his cheek.

"I've never found an adequate definition for it," Mikhail returned. "All I can go on is my feelings and the fact that I've not been able to put you from my mind—not even into one isolated corner of it. You're right there in plain sight. I've never felt toward anyone as I do about you right now."

"Right now?" she questioned before another kiss. "And after this moment?"

"There will be many, many more, dearest Jennifer, many, many more." One last kiss and Mikhail put the car into motion.

Dinner was superb. The concert was exciting. The pianist brilliant, the orchestra splendid. Still, after an already long day, Jennifer felt as if she were beginning to grow weary.

The party after, while interesting, proved exhausting to her. Mikhail was recognized and constantly being pulled into little clusters of conversation. He tugged her along.

Finally, when Mikhail and the pianist who had performed that evening went into a huddle, Jennifer edged away from the crowd and found a seat.

The waddling, rotund figure of Lionel Adams approached her in his customary flamboyant attire, glasses half slipped down his nose as he eyed her over them. "I know we must have met last week after my little recital, but my memory isn't the best with names. Faces yes, names so-so."

"Jennifer Logan. I was Mrs. Margarethe Watts' guest at your concert," she replied.

"Oh yes, I recall. May I sit?" He did so with a grunt. "I love these things, but they can be perfectly tiring after a while." He chuckled and stared at her for a few moments. "Ah yes, so you're the one."

"The one *what?*"

"The one *who*, my dear," Lionel corrected. "To be specific, the one who has captured Mikhail's heart. When he played this afternoon at his session, I realized that a tremendous change had come over him—to put it bluntly, that he had fallen in love."

Jennifer smiled and felt her face become flushed.

"I don't object—far from it," Lionel continued. "I think it's wonderful. Every creative artist should be in love; it makes so much difference in his output and interpretation. Mikhail has presented several girls to me for my approval in the past. Quite frankly, I tried to be kind, but it was difficult. I nearly ended up with a bloody tongue from biting it so much. Oh, I suppose they were nice enough in their ways and they tickled his fancy for the moment. Generally, I found them vacuous and alien to art circles. When I saw you briefly at Margarethe's house last Saturday, and we didn't get a chance to chat, I perceived that Mikhail was quite interested in you."

"I was a little like a fish out of water," Jennifer admitted.

"Not at all." Lionel adjusted himself and reached for a glass of punch from a passing tray. "Margarethe showed me one of your pictures. I realized in an instant that you had artistic talent, probably greater potential than you realize. I considered it a small masterpiece."

"You're exaggerating."

"That's my prerogative as an eccentric individual, Miss Logan. Allow me that." Lionel cleared his throat. "What I'm trying to say is that I've always felt Mikhail would never find true happiness with a woman unless she were artistically inclined and had the mind of a creative person. It would take that type to even begin to understand Mikhail's genius. On top of that, you're very pretty. Why, you could even become a photographer's model, I should imagine, and do quite well at it."

"That's hardly where my interests lie."

"Do you love Mikhail?"

Jennifer considered the question. "Yes."

"Are you in love with him?"

"Isn't that the same thing?"

"No, no, my dear, loving someone is quite different from being in love with him. I love all my students, but I'm not in love with any of them. I love many people I'm not actually in love with," Lionel explained. "One only falls in love with that special someone who means everything to him."

"In that case, I believe I may be falling in love with Mikhail."

"*Brava! Brava!*" Lionel cheered. "I'm delighted to hear that. I hope you go all the way and fall completely in love with him without reservations. He needs that, you know. An artist too consumed in himself can become self-destructive in time. An artist in love—ah, that's another matter! I pray you will discover that you have fallen fully in love with him and let him know it before he flies off to New York for those all-important auditions. It can make a vast difference in his performance."

"Flies to New York?"

"Hasn't he told you? Oh dear, I may have let the pussy out." Lionel's jowls shook as he twisted his face. "Well, since it is—and don't you dare tell him I told you—Cleo Dennison has arranged for him to play before some very important people in New York music circles. If he passes that acid test, he may well be on his way to a successful concert tour."

New York, Jennifer thought as Lionel trudged away from her on the pretense of having to speak with the orchestra conductor before he left.

A smartly dressed woman in a designer creation, neither short nor tall, with an attractive face, had been watching Jennifer throughout the course of the party. Their eyes had met on more than one occasion. The woman had busied about in conversation with many different people, indicating that she was well acquainted. She was one who stood out in a crowd. It would have been difficult for Jennifer to judge her age. She could have been anywhere between forty and sixty, with a vivacious quality that proved age was not important.

As Jennifer rose from where she had been seated speaking with Lionel Adams, the distinguished woman headed in her direction. A soft hand was extended to her. "I'm Vivian Nelson. How do you do? I've been observing you."

"I've noticed. I'm Jennifer Logan." At close range, she could see that Vivian Nelson was perhaps a few years older than she had originally guessed she might be.

"You seemed to be attached with rather binding glue to Mikhail Alexander earlier," Vivian said. "How did you ever manage to tug your way free of him? Don't tell me. He finally found someone with whom he could speak intensely about music, isn't that the case? You're a lovely beauty. You need have no fear—he'll be back for you. Do you smoke?"

"No, thank you."

Vivian fumbled in a case for a cigarette. "I do occasionally. Do you drink?"

"I've had some punch, thank you." Jennifer had begun to feel uneasy.

"I was alluding to something a little stronger," Vivian said as she used a gold lighter to light her cigarette. "I don't inhale. Just like to puff a bit and hold them. Everyone smokes in art circles; I feel I should every now and then." She laughed. "Denver has its share of art patrons. I number myself among them. While I think Mikhail is brilliant, and I do love concerts, my forte is more with painters, sculptors and their ilk. Mikhail has talent in that direction, too."

"You sound as if you know him quite well," Jennifer remarked.

Vivian laughed loudly. "When a person has only one grandson, she makes a point of knowing him quite well."

"You're—?" Jennifer could not hide an expression of astonishment.

"I understand he coerced you into wearing that dreadful pale blue bathing suit of mine," Vivian added. "I trust he had more difficulty coaxing you out of it."

"You're his grandmother?"

"Good God, not so loud!" Vivian reprimanded. "I prefer that people think of me only as Mikhail's close relative."

Jennifer laughed and began to relax.

"My daughter's his mother," Vivian continued. "I usually try to pass for her sister." She reached for Jennifer's hand. "I'm having a game with you, my dear. I'm really terribly pleased that I'm Mikhail's grandmother. Admittedly, however, I don't always try to act my age." She studied Jennifer's face. "You like him very much, don't you?"

"Yes."

"Then go for him," Vivian stated. "He's a prize. I don't say that just because he's my kin. He needs to truly love and be loved. Doesn't everyone? Mikhail especially needs it. He was extremely close to his grandfather—my husband. When he passed away nearly five years ago, Mikhail felt it greatly. He had dated previous to that. After his grandfather's death, he changed, got a little wild and reckless. When I gave him Largo a year later, I had hoped he'd return to his old ways. Yet I knew from the type of girls he would bring around that he was only in the business of sowing wild oats, and I feared he might begin to neglect his piano. Fortunately, he always had his friend Philip nearby to help him out of sticky messes."

"Sticky messes?"

"Mixing with the wrong people." Vivian stared into space. "Mikhail's changed in the last six months to a year. He told me last spring that he wanted to become serious about his life and his concert career. I instinctively knew that he would start seeking out a different kind of lady. The wild oats scene had grown old and he craved something with more substance. He wants you, you know."

"He told you so?"

"We had quite a talk here midweek. He usually comes by my place once a week for supper, or he takes me out," Vivian explained. "He confided in me that he was falling in love. He couldn't explain how or why it was happening, except that he had been seeing a face in his mind or his dreams or those peculiar trances he puts himself into while he plays. Suddenly, you materialized and he's falling in love. Sounds like a romantic fantasy, doesn't it? That was my first impression. He wanted me to meet you here tonight, on my own, without introduction from anyone else. He wanted my impression."

"I hope you are pleased."

"Well pleased, my dear Jennifer, well pleased." Vivian patted her arm. "You'll have your hands full with him. I did with his grandfather . . . and my husband was much older than

Mikhail when we married. Be patient and you'll be able to mold him. I did."

"Thank you, Mrs. Nelson."

"Never mind the Mrs. Nelson bit," Vivian said, "I'm just plain Vivian. We'll have to have a look at your artwork one of these days. I have connections; maybe I can arrange an exhibit of your work."

"It's not for showing. I'm really preparing to be an illustrator."

"I can help you find a place for that, too." Vivian put her hands to Jennifer's shoulders and kissed her cheek. "I'm very pleased to know you, Jennifer."

Jennifer had difficulty keeping her eyes open on the way to Largo. Once they left the city with the bright lights and noises, the blackness around seemed to envelop her. Finally, she gave in to drowsiness and napped part of the way.

Mikhail stroked her arm and gently shook her awake as he prepared to turn off the main highway. She awakened to the muffled click-clack of the windshield wipers.

Mikhail's hand clasped hers. "It's raining. The road from here on out can be a little bumpy and sloshy."

"How long did I sleep?"

"From there to here—wherever there was." Mikhail laughed. "I'm sorry I kept you out so late. Maybe we should have stayed in the city. I wanted you to see morning—rainy or not—at Largo."

"I'm sorry. I must have been terrible company."

"Not at all. I enjoyed just being in the car with you," Mikhail said. "Vivian says you got a 100 on the test."

"Which test?"

"Her test. She likes you."

Mikhail saw Jennifer into the house before he went back to unload the car.

"Better take a warm shower," Mikhail said, "and hop into bed. You can have the room next to mine. Doubt if Philip will be here tonight."

"The room next to yours?" Jennifer questioned.

"Follow me." Mikhail led the way, carrying her luggage.

After a warm refreshing shower, Jennifer slipped into her nightie and robe and adjourned to the assigned bedroom. She could hear the shower water running. For a few moments she fought sleep. Then as she was about to lose the battle, Mikhail came padding into the room. He sat on the bed and ran his fingers over her face.

"Thanks for being with me tonight," Mikhail said as he lowered his face to kiss her lips. "Pleasant dreams." He tucked the covers before he kissed her again, turned out the light and went through the door leading to his room.

Jennifer's eyes popped open. Suddenly, she was wide awake. Once the light was extinguished in Mikhail's room, she threw the covers back. It was another several seconds before she worked up the nerve to sit up and finally stand. For a few moments more she bolstered her courage and then crossed in the direction of his room.

"Mikhail?" she said softly at the side of his bed.

"Yes?" He turned on the light beside him, the dimmer switch at low. "What is it?"

Jennifer stood trembling. "I want—I want to sleep with you —if you don't mind."

"Are you sure?"

"Positive." She reached down to pull the covers back.

"I don't wear pajamas."

"In that case," Jennifer said as she pulled the straps of her nightie over her shoulders and let it slide down her body, "neither will I." She sat on the bed and waited for his arm around her before she stretched out and pressed tightly against him.

CHAPTER EIGHT

Jennifer's life changed drastically after that weekend with Mikhail. Falling deeply in love with him and he with her was the easy part. They fit well together and found great satisfaction with each other. He opened a way to a new aspect of life for her, and she gave him a kind of fulfillment he had never received from any other woman. The very act of being in love was a new dimension for each of them.

By that Sunday evening there was no doubt in either of their minds that they belonged together.

"There's something I must tell you," Mikhail said when the kitchen was straightened after dinner and he caught her in a tight hug.

"What? That you've fallen out of love with me already?" She teased.

"No. I'll never do that," he replied. "Come into the den where I've a fire blazing."

"One kiss."

Mikhail kissed her with aching lips and she responded with her body tightly against his.

"Okay, what's this big revelation?" Jennifer asked as they settled comfortably on the cushions near the fire.

"Cleo Dennison wants me to go to New York as soon as possible," Mikhail announced, watching her face for reaction.

"How soon? When . . . ?" Jennifer asked. Fortunately, she had been forewarned that the trip was necessary and important to his career.

"Philip's dance program is next Friday night," Mikhail said. "I can't miss that. But I promised I would fly out Saturday morning. Cleo had to juggle an audition she'd set up for Friday."

"Then by all means, you must go." Jennifer smiled approval. "I've never asked. Can you drive?"

"Yes. I've had a license since I was sixteen."

"Good. Then you can drive me to the airport and have the car for your use while I'm gone," he said, again beginning to nibble kisses.

"Maybe it would be best if I checked out of Larchmont," Jennifer suggested. "If I have your car, I can drive back and forth for the few classes I have."

"Great idea!" he agreed. "Where will you stay? I wouldn't want you to be here by yourself."

"I should be able to arrange something."

Mikhail snapped his fingers. "I've just the thing. There's a small apartment where Vivian lives. She would love to have you close by, and it would be an opportunity for both of you to get to know each other better."

"I don't have much money of my own," she said. "Perhaps I can convince my father to help me out."

"Never mind about that. I've money and, if worse comes to worst, I'm certain Vivian will help out."

Mikhail called his grandmother and made certain the small apartment was still available.

"She's absolutely wild about the idea," he said a few minutes later after hanging up. "In fact it's the best news she's had in days. Once you know her, getting acquainted with my mother will be easy. However, let me warn you, you'll have to charm the socks off of Dad. The only thing you have to remember with him, he occasionally likes to think of himself as a Russian bear—white Russian, of course. He likes to growl and snarl. I'm certain you'll have him around your little finger in no time."

Further plans were made as they snuggled by the fire.

"I really don't want to go back to Larchmont tonight," Jennifer said as the hour grew late.

"No point in unnecessarily rattling cages there," he replied. "I'll make arrangements tomorrow morning for the apartment and have my regular coaching session with Lionel in the afternoon. I'll pick you up in the evening and we can start transferring your things."

"Do you think I can move in that soon?"

"If not, you can leave stuff at Vivian's. Bring your artwork first, she'll want to see it." Mikhail laughed as he embraced her and forced another series of exotic kisses.

The headmistress at Larchmont was receptive to Jennifer's plan, since they were short on living space and three girls had to share one room, where two was the accepted number. She told Jennifer that she had hoped she would make other arrangements, but that they would never ask her to leave since she had been a student for such a long time.

"Are you going to live with him?" Pauline asked as Jennifer packed her drawings and art supplies.

"Not yet." She explained the situation.

"I'll miss you."

"How can you miss me? I'll be taking my classes as usual. We'll see each other practically every day."

"It won't be the same, sharing the room with someone else," Pauline moaned with a dramatic flair. "I suppose it was inevitable. Here, let me help you."

Mikhail arrived at five minutes after five. The car was loaded by five-thirty.

"I'll probably have only three suitcases and a few small boxes," Jennifer explained as he held the car door for her. "I gave away a lot of clothes I no longer wear."

Mikhail kissed her fervently before he started the car. "Good news. You can be in the apartment tomorrow. The owner wants to tidy up and air it out." He held her hand as they drove. "Incidentally, I received another call from Cleo today. She's really lining things up for me in New York. Guess she's a real go-getter."

"I'm sorry I didn't get better acquainted with her the night of the recital, when we briefly spoke," Jennifer said.

Vivian Nelson wore slacks and a blouse hanging outside when she went to the door to greet her grandson and Jennifer. She welcomed them each warmly with a kiss and a patronizing hug. "Sorry I couldn't have it for you today, Jenni, but they did a little touch up painting."

"No hurry. I plan to stay at Larchmont for the rest of the week."

Mikhail and Jennifer unloaded the car and put the things in Vivian's quaintly attractive apartment.

"Yes, I like this," Vivian praised when Jennifer displayed her artwork a while later. "You've talent, young lady, a great deal of it. Illustration would be very good for you, although I must say some of your individual creative art is extremely salable, too."

Mikhail was equally impressed. "You didn't tell me you were this good."

"How could I tell you? You had to see for yourself, and this is the first opportunity you've had," Jennifer replied, proud of the approval.

"In fact, I have a friend who has a small gallery here in Denver," Vivian added. "We'll have a few of these pieces framed and have him hang them for you. If he sells them on commission, you'll be ahead of the game. If not, nothing will be lost but a little time in preparing them."

"Do you really think they're good enough to be shown?"

"Look, kiddo, I've been around art circles for more years than I care to count. I've even sponsored artists with half the talent you have. You're wasting your time at Larchmont. You should have been studying privately with one or more of several excellent teachers—who just happen to be my friends. We'll get onto that once you've moved in and settled."

After they had light refreshments with Vivian, Mikhail drove her back to Larchmont. They parked a short distance from the school.

"Second thoughts?" Mikhail asked after he had kissed her and held her in a firm embrace.

"About what?"

"Leaving Larchmont."

"No. The sooner the better. Both you and Vivian have inspired me to do something about my art."

"What about second thoughts about me?"

"Second, third and fourth—and they're all positive and in your favor," Jennifer assured him. "I wish we were spending the night together."

"You know I've fallen crazily in love with you, don't you?" Mikhail said before he kissed her.

"Do you think I haven't fallen in love with you?" she asked.

"I think maybe you have."

"Only *maybe?*" She dove toward his face and aggressively kissed him. "I've come out of my shell, sweetheart, and I unequivocably know what I want—and who." She kissed him again.

The following night Mikhail moved all but one small bag from Larchmont and later helped Jennifer prepare things in her new apartment.

"I've arranged for you to have a phone installed tomorrow," Mikhail said while they relaxed on the sofa. "Vivian will be here to see that it's properly connected. And tomorrow night I think we'd better make a point of meeting your parents. It's time I knew them."

"They're not the easiest people to know," Jennifer advised. "They have their peculiarities."

"Is that some kind of warning?" Mikhail laughed and kissed her.

"You'll see for yourself." Jennifer ran her hand over his chest. "Going to spend the night?"

"I wouldn't miss it for the world." Mikhail pulled her to him. "About that 'early to bed, early to rise' adage." His words filled her mouth and she nodded consent.

The Logan family home was located in the older wealthy section of Denver. A concrete wall with iron stake fence kept intruders out. The well-trimmed lawn of summer now had only a faint green tint as it gave way to the golden brown of autumn. Several below-freezing nights had turned the leaves. An austere attitude prevailed.

Wind swept leaves across the lawn as the car pulled through the gates and up the circular drive to the large red-brick and stone structure. The shades had been drawn and faint light shone through two on the first floor and one on the second.

"They're conservative," Jennifer said, "they don't use a lot of light. Many of the rooms have already been shut off to conserve heat. You'll see. Brace yourself."

Jennifer let herself in the main entrance. The foyer was dimly lit by one small antique lamp. Prudence Logan met them at the parlor door. She wore no makeup and her hair had been self-styled in an awkward upsweep. Mikhail could see Jennifer's features in her mother's face.

"Mother, may I present Mikhail Alexander. My mother, Mrs. Logan," Jennifer introduced.

"How do you do, Mr. Alexander." Prudence's words were crisp and edged with coldness. "Won't you come in?"

Jennifer led the way into the parlor and stopped short as she beheld her grandmother sitting imperiously in the Queen Anne chair. "Oh!" She hesitated before she pulled Mikhail toward the older woman. "Grandmother Logan, may I present Mikhail Alexander? My grandmother, Mrs. Logan."

Old Mrs. Logan held her position without batting an eyelash. Her pursed lips finally moved from side to side as if she were sucking on a mint. She slowly nodded her head in recognition.

Clarence Logan, tall, slender and balding, had stood when they entered. He wore a cardigan sweater over a starched shirt and a tie. Glasses gave his eyes a curious appearance. "How do you do, Mr. Alexander? I'm Jennifer's father."

"You're an entertainer, aren't you, Mr. Alexander?" Old Mrs. Logan inserted and again gave that sucking mint quality to her mouth.

"Mikhail is a concert pianist," Jennifer said.

"You perform in front of people, don't you?" Mrs. Logan asked.

"Yes."

"Then he's an entertainer," the old lady snapped.

"Won't you have a seat, Mr. Alexander?" Prudence asked. "I'll bring tea and biscuits." Her whispered movements rustled from the room.

"Don't go to any trouble on my behalf," Mikhail called.

Jennifer sat in a chair close to the one Mikhail had taken.

"Are you in business, Mr. Alexander?" Clarence inquired as he returned to his seat.

"I'm a musician. My father is Ivan Alexander of Alexander

Construction," Mikhail replied. "You have a charming place here."

"Never mind the charming place, young man," Mrs. Logan bit. "It's been in the family for generations. Is your father's business successful?"

"Really, Mother," Clarence interrupted. "I don't believe it is necessary to bring that up at this juncture."

"I don't expect to stay up all night, Clarence," Mrs. Logan stated. "I want to know what this young upstart is all about."

Mikhail began to bristle. "My father's business is most successful, Mrs. Logan. I am his only son and heir. I didn't bring a financial statement with me, but I assure you my father is wealthy enough to have built his own modern house with a lawn more spacious than yours. They have one live-in servant and two who come in to clean. Our family car is a Rolls-Royce, Mother has a Jaguar and Dad drives around in a Cadillac. I am a musician by choice but, were I ever to deem it necessary, I could easily work alongside my father. My mother's maiden name is Nelson. My grandfather was a well-known architect."

"That seems adequate," the old lady commented. "However, I'm still not in favor of my granddaughter seeing an entertainer."

"Really, Mother, do get off of that. I assure you there's quite a difference between a concert pianist and what you consider an entertainer," Clarence said without raising his voice.

"Then you approve of Jennifer consorting with this type of person?" Mrs. Logan questioned.

"I certainly don't disapprove."

Prudence arrived with the tray of tea and cookies, which she insisted on calling biscuits. Silence prevailed as she poured and Jennifer dispensed the teacups and saucers.

"The next time I play a concert in Denver," Mikhail said to break the mordant silence, "I would like you all to attend. Then you'll see the kind of entertainer I am."

"He's excellent," Jennifer interjected. "Even you would like his playing, Grandmother."

"I'm not so sure of that," Mrs. Logan snipped.

"I believe you'll change your opinion once you've heard him."

"As you well know, Jennifer," the old lady said, "I rarely alter my opinion. I haven't perpetuated the Logan fortune in the stock market by changing my mind at every turn and whim."

"I dare say you've had your share of disappointments by clinging to such stubborn tenacity," Mikhail interjected. "My father has always taught me that adaptability is the keystone to progress in business."

"Quite so," Clarence muttered and shot a cautious eye in Mrs. Logan's direction.

"Don't side with him, Clarence. You know my feelings about such matters." Mrs. Logan frowned and twisted her lips. "I think I've had quite enough tea and inane conversation. It must be getting on toward nine and I don't wish to miss the news."

Prudence quickly moved to assist Mrs. Logan from the chair.

"Let me help," Jennifer volunteered.

Supported between daughter-in-law and granddaughter, Mrs. Logan glared curiously at Mikhail as he stood.

"It's been a pleasure meeting you, Mrs. Logan."

"It has *not*. I'm not a pleasant person to know, Mr. Alexander. I pride myself on being cantankerous." A faint light came to her eye along with a singular wisp of a twisted smile. She nodded and motioned to be assisted from the room.

Mikhail tried not to sigh noticeably with relief.

"Help yourself to more tea," Clarence offered. "I'll have a bit more myself."

Mikhail poured, attempting to avoid direct eye contact with Clarence. He glanced in the direction the ladies had gone before he sat. "With all due respect, I would guess your mother could practically romp up those stairs if she didn't want the attention."

Clarence at first looked shocked, then he smiled. "You may well be correct in that assessment. I often suspect she plays the feeble role for a purpose." He sugared his tea. "I was a small child when my father left. He ran off with a show girl, managed to get his hands on a substantial amount of the Logan money and just disappeared. My mother has been vehement toward entertainers ever since."

"A concert pianist and a show girl are nowhere in the same category, Mr. Logan."

"Oh, I'm well aware of that." Clarence chuckled as he

thought. "Frankly, I've always thought that my father actually just had a fling with the girl, since he had probably long been looking for an escape. If you think Jennifer's grandmother is difficult, you should have known my grandmother. Had I been a different type of person and possessed a little more backbone, I might have fled, too. I've been motivated by a strong sense of security, hammered into me by my mother and grandmother. It was safer to remain here and live a docile existence." He sighed deeply. "Sometimes I wish it had been different. I've become accustomed to habit. Not having been blessed with a prodigious libido—or is 'cursed' the proper word—I have found comfort in simple pleasures."

"I suppose you have a stamp collection," Mikhail said facetiously.

"Stamps *and* coins. I once became caught up in butterflies, but that proved too time-consuming and Mother disapproved." He stared into the teacup. "What are your intentions concerning Jennifer?"

"I'm in love with her."

"Implying—?"

"That by today's standards, my intentions are extremely good," Mikhail stated. "However, according to Victorian mores —well, I live today, not then."

"I see." Clarence glanced up. "I do read, you know, most voraciously. I don't always like what I read about contemporary attitudes. I would certainly never permit Jennifer to attend a coeducational school, especially one of so-called higher learning where they allow members of the opposite sexes to share dormitories. That is completely inconceivable to me."

"I question your opinion of your libido, Mr. Logan."

"I beg your pardon?"

"It may not be prodigious, but I suspect you've simply suppressed that which was natural for you—probably at the insistence of your mother and grandmother. If your father was such a—if I may use archaic words—bounder and philanderer, I fail to see how you avoided inheriting some of his characteristics. Or perhaps those libidinous traits became dormant for a generation and resurfaced with Jennifer."

Clarence bit his lip. "I have learned to control such appetites."

"And grown old and negatively opinionated long before your time," Mikhail asserted. "Fine, if that suits you. As to Jennifer, I'm very much in love with her. When the time is right, I intend to marry her—with or without your blessings, sir. Artists are dissimilar from practical business people. We have a way of expressing life differently. I might add, Jennifer is also very much an artist, extremely talented."

"Yes, I know she is," Clarence admitted. He emptied his teacup. "Most of what you have said is true, I reluctantly have to admit—I mean about me, even about my father, although I hardly knew him. His name was Atwater. I was born an Atwater, but after his departure, Mother insisted on resuming her maiden name and mine was legally changed to Logan. I often dreamed that I would one day encounter John Atwater, just to see what kind of a person he really was. I might not have been disappointed."

Mikhail rose and stepped to the chair to put his hand on Clarence's shoulder. "Please stand."

Clarence hesitantly stood and reacted with stunned surprise when Mikhail wrapped his arms about him and held him close.

"Don't fight me, Mr. Logan. Love me as a son."

Clarence tightened his embrace. When he stepped back, he had to remove his glasses to wipe them. "I'll try."

"Shall I make another pot of tea?" Prudence asked when she returned with her daughter.

"It's late, Mother," Jennifer said.

Mikhail stepped to Jennifer and firmly took her hand. "We must be going. Entertainer or not, a concert pianist must adhere to a strict discipline." He shook Prudence's hand. "It's been enlightening meeting you, Mrs. Logan. Perhaps next time I will be less a stranger."

"I do hope so, Mr. Alexander."

"Mr. Logan . . ." He disconnected his hand from Jennifer's long enough to shake Clarence's and pat him on the shoulder. "We'll become better acquainted, too."

"Yes, I'm certain of that." Clarence cast a cautious glance at Prudence.

Both Mr. and Mrs. Logan saw the young couple to the door.

"Whew!" Mikhail exclaimed as he slid behind the wheel of the car. "That was a scene!"

"I warned you it might be an ordeal." Jennifer squeezed his hand. "I think you've won my father. That's a major step. Grandmother will never change, so why worry about it?"

The car pulled out of the driveway into the street.

"Mother told me she thought you were very nice—and extremely handsome. And she loved the way you stood up to Grandmother."

"I'll bet she's been wanting to tell the old girl off for years," Mikhail said. "Someday we'll have to have your parents out to Largo. I might even persuade your father to go skinny-dipping in the pool with me. And we may be able to coerce your mother into Vivian's pale blue bikini."

"I wouldn't push it there," Jennifer returned with laughter.

"I would guess that your grandmother and Vivian are pretty much close to the same age. Isn't it amazing what opinions and attitudes do to people?" Mikhail asked as he reached to make physical contact with Jennifer.

CHAPTER NINE

Philip Franklin danced the leading role in *The Afternoon of a Faun* with such sensuous characterization and technique that he received a standing ovation. The audience called for more, but he left them wanting.

"I had no idea that Philip was so talented," Jennifer said after the houselights came up.

"He's my little brother, and I couldn't be prouder of him," Mikhail exclaimed. "We're actually like that, you know—the two artistic kids on the block, etcetera."

"He told me you two were ostracized by the other kids because of your talent." Jennifer held tightly to Mikhail's hand.

"We were the lucky ones, although we didn't think so at the time. Quite the opposite. Let's go backstage and congratulate him."

Jennifer and Mikhail attended the party afterward but did not stay late because of his early flight plans the next day.

"I wish we could have spent this last night together at Largo," Mikhail said much later in Jennifer's darkened apartment. "It's not that I don't like it here, it's fine—and anywhere with you is beautiful. I'd just like to be there with you. Largo is special to me—almost as special as you are."

Jennifer held tight to him. "I don't want to let you go."

"It's best if I travel alone this time," Mikhail insisted. "Once I have a sense of the city and make the right connections, then it will be different. You're liable to feel neglected while I'm busy mingling in musical circles."

"You don't think I will feel that way, waiting for you here?"

"You mustn't react like that, Jenni. We can't either of us stand in the way of the other's progress. We have each other, but we each have our own individual interests and careers."

"I'll try to learn. It won't be easy." Jennifer sighed and kissed him with all the love that was in her.

Although it was not initially planned that way, Cleo Dennison arranged for Mikhail to be busy in New York for a full month. He played a dozen auditions and, as a result, performed a miniconcert for a selected group of critics and music patrons. The patrons for the most part were overwhelmingly enthusiastic; the critics had their opinions and suggestions.

"I want to arrange a Carnegie Hall recital for you," Cleo said, "to see how others will respond. I have backing for you, and your sponsors foresee an excellent career ahead of you."

"I've you to thank for that," Mikhail said as he sat across from her at the Russian Tea Room. "I can't believe all you've done for me so far."

"I'll do more in time, Mikhail, believe me." Cleo stared fondly into his handsome face. "I'll have recording companies represented at your Carnegie debut. These things take a little time. I have confidence."

"Thanks."

"I wish you didn't have to return to Denver," Cleo said later. "It would be nice if you could take an apartment here in New York where you would be close at hand."

"There's a hand I want to be close to in Denver," he replied.

"Oh? I hadn't realized." Cleo raised an eyebrow and assumed a sophisticated expression.

"You told me I shouldn't mix my personal with my professional life," Mikhail reminded her. "I've taken that advice to heart."

Cleo looked away and scratched for a cigarette from her bag. "I see." She forced a smile. "That is how it should be."

"I'm planning to marry." Mikhail watched for her further reaction.

Cleo breathed deeply. "I think that wise—providing your wife-to-be doesn't mind remaining in the background. Don't misunderstand. I think it'll be wonderful for you to have a personal outlet, someone to go home to. I even encourage that with my gay performers. Simply don't flaunt your private life—not until you're well established. Okay, so some *grande dame* gets the hots for you. Politely tell her about your wife and let her know you're not interested in a personal dalliance. Fine! I think that's great."

"Do you?" He stared deeply into her eyes.

Cleo glanced away. "Of course."

"But you're disappointed."

Cleo smiled and shook her head. "Not really. Our arrangement is strictly business, Mikhail. You're a product which I intend to sell. If the ultimate results make you rich and famous, then I'll profit from it as well. And profit for me means survival. That's all."

"What about personal feelings?" he asked.

"Detachment's the name of the game," she said, forcing herself to maintain a fixed smile. "Once, several years ago, I handled an artist who had remarkable talent. He had many assets worth promoting. Unfortunately, due to my inexperience, I took a very personal interest in him and led with unchecked emotions. I didn't realize that he and the man he lived with were anything more than roommates. I had a rude awakening, reacted with a vengeance and dropped him like a hot potato. It took me a long time to get over him. Ironically, another manager picked him up almost instantly and propelled him into a fantastically successful career. I resolved then that I would never allow myself to get emotionally involved with any of my clients. And I've done my best to remain objective ever since. Period. End of chapter."

"Thanks for telling me that," Mikhail said with an understanding smile.

During the month in New York, Mikhail wrote letters to Jennifer practically every day and she immediately answered them. After two weeks she began to perceive a noticeable change in the tone of what he wrote. In a way she was a little annoyed that he so often mentioned Cleo and the things they did together, such as going to the theater and attending concerts. To conquer doubts in her own mind, Jennifer expressed her innermost feelings in the letters, pouring out her soul to him.

On the lighter side, she related that two of her paintings had sold at the gallery and she had been encouraged to paint additional ones. She also said that she and Vivian had become very close and that Vivian had helped her to make contact with several publishers to do freelance illustrations. Furthermore, she was studying with a prominent art teacher who was assisting her to develop a style uniquely her own and she had begun to work with oils.

"Why don't you come to the airport with me, Vivian?" Jennifer asked as she prepared to meet Mikhail's plane.

"No, my dear Jenni, this is a time when you and my grandson should be alone together," Vivian replied. "After all, he's been away from you longer than you've actually known him. You need as much time together as you can possibly have."

"Guess I just felt like I needed some moral support."

"Mikhail will give you all of that you need," Vivian assured her. "I know my grandson too well. I don't want him to think that I am in any way interfering."

Jennifer kissed Vivian and thanked her.

"Oh God, I'm glad to be home!" Mikhail exclaimed as he passionately hugged Jennifer at the airport. "More than that, it's absolutely wonderful to have my arms around you again."

"Oh, I know, I know!" Jennifer replied as any doubts she might have had were dispelled. "Shall we go directly out to Largo?"

"Hey, you're as anxious as I am, aren't you?"

"Passion allegro."

Mikhail hugged and kissed her again. "Honey, I'm all for that. However, I'd like to stop on the way for dinner and relax over wine before we head home. I picked at what they served on the flight and did my stomach a favor by not eating it."

"I'm with you."

"I know—and I love it." Another kiss. "But let's get out of here before we attract a crowd of voyeurs." He pulled her toward the baggage pickup station. "I know just the place. And it's on the way to Largo. Quiet and isolated. I'll call ahead for reservations. It's very popular because it has little nooks and crannies with candlelit semiprivacy."

"Sounds super!" Jennifer exclaimed. "I'll wait for your luggage while you call."

"That's taken care of," Mikhail reported a short while later when he returned to where Jennifer was waiting at the baggage carousel.

"Thought you had more than two suitcases."

"I left the rest of the things in New York—at Cleo's place," Mikhail said. "Stuff I don't necessarily need but I'll want when I return to New York."

"Will that be soon?" Jennifer asked as they walked to where the car was parked.

"I'll probably be going back and forth periodically," he replied. "May even have to take a small apartment in Manhattan. It'll be cheaper than staying in hotels."

"Oh." Jennifer tried not to sound disappointed.

The Golden Pony was located on the highway, somewhat remote, but extremely popular. They were immediately shown to their table at a window in the corner. After they were situated, Mikhail ordered a martini. Jennifer preferred only water.

"You order for me," she said, unable to make a selection from the menu.

"Fine. And wine?"

"I'll have wine with supper," she replied and stared questioningly at his martini.

"Cleo got me into the martini habit," Mikhail explained. "She always had two before dinner. It helps me relax. Sure you won't have one?"

"Positive."

After the second martini, while still waiting to be served, Mikhail reached across the table and handed her a glass of wine. "Jenni, I have something very important to say to you."

"Which is?"

"I love you very much—and I'm very much in love with you. I know that now more than ever." He raised his glass to her. "And I have an equally important question to ask you."

"Yes?"

"Will you marry me? I want to share my entire life with you. Take time to think about your answer."

"I've been thinking about my answer all the time you were away. Yes—yes, yes—yes!"

Mikhail pulled her close and kissed her. "Oh, Jenni, I want us to be so very happy together."

"So do I."

"Maybe I should have waited until after supper to ask, but I couldn't hold it any longer," he said. "Hope it won't spoil your appetite."

"My appetite is for you, wherever you are, whatever you do," she replied. "But I may have difficulty concentrating on food."

The waiter interrupted their eye-gazing romantic mood to serve.

"I want to get married as soon as possible," Mikhail said during the course of the meal. "I mean, like tonight, if we could find someone to marry us. I don't want a lot of pomp and ceremony."

"What about my parents—and yours?" Jennifer asked.

"We'll marry and tell them later."

"Aren't you rushing things?"

"You don't want to marry me right away?"

"Couldn't we wait at least until tomorrow?" Jennifer returned, holding tightly to his hand.

"Well—no later." Mikhail laughed and poured more wine. "I'll call Philip to stand with me. What about Pauline Maples?"

"She'd love it. We may have to squeeze it between her classes," Jennifer replied merrily.

The wedding took place three days later to comply with state laws. Instead of the small, intimate affair Mikhail had proposed, the ceremony took place in a chapel with a few invited guests. After the couple threatened to elope without their approval, Clarence and Prudence attended sans Grandmother Logan. The Alexanders were present, with Vivian in charge of arrangements. A few friends were invited, and, of course, Lionel Adams and Maynard Weiskoff, as well as Margarethe Watts and some of her friends.

"I thought you said simple and quiet," Pauline remarked as she stood beside Jennifer in the reception line.

"Some things get out of control," Jennifer replied. "Enjoy it, Pauline."

"I just ask one favor—be sure you toss me the bouquet."

Philip proudly remained at Mikhail's side, although when he was initially told about the arrangements, he entertained serious doubts about it. Mikhail tried to convince his friend that it would be great for him. Jennifer would be living at Largo where she could have the studio for her artwork, and he could get back to long hours of practice. As far as Philip was concerned, he would always be welcome in their home and nothing would change. He could use the basement studio as usual.

"I do wish you two had given me a tad more time to really arrange a gala affair," Vivian complained, "but we'll make do."

The reception was held at the Alexander home. While the Logans felt out of place in the elegant modern setting, they did their best to mingle with the guests. Margarethe Watts made a special point of making them feel welcome since she had made their acquaintance in the past. Constance Alexander graciously gave Prudence Logan a tour of the house while Ivan Alexander did his pompous best to strike up a cordial conversation with Clarence Logan. Despite their differences, the two fathers found they had some things in common.

Pauline Maples was up front and Jennifer made a point of throwing the bouquet directly at her. "Oh my God! I actually caught it. Now if you can just find a man to toss with it."

"Problems?" Mikhail asked when he approached Philip, who was standing on the sidelines wearing a glum expression.

"No." Philip shook his handsome head. "Guess it all happened so fast—I wasn't prepared for it. I had always envisioned us both going to New York and sharing a place while we tried to get our feet in the right doors. You've already got both feet in and I haven't even started."

"Is that what's really bothering you, buddy-boy?" Mikhail threw his arm around Philip's shoulders.

"I love Jenni," Philip said, "and I love you, too. You're my big brother. I don't know—guess I just thought you wouldn't marry so soon. I know you say I'll always be welcome at Largo—but now I'll sort of be the odd man out, a third shoe."

"Things won't really change between us now," Mikhail assured him. "We'll still have our long chats, work out dance routines, swim—when I'm home. Maybe you and Jenni can get better acquainted when I have to go out of town." He tousled

Philip's hair. "We both had to grow up eventually—but we'll always be friends."

"Okay, you two," Vivian said as she joined them. "Enough of this standing around on the sidelines. Since the groom is supposed to have the first dance with the bride, I'll have it with Philip."

A small combo had been playing background music. When they broke into a lively number, Mikhail went to Jennifer. As soon as they began dancing, Vivian grabbed hold of Philip and whirled him onto the floor.

"What say you and I make a surprise trip to New York when Mikhail makes his Carnegie Hall debut?" Vivian asked as she danced with Philip. "I've still got a few bucks in my piggy bank. It'll be my treat. Besides, you may not realize it, but this spring —well, midsummer—chicken knows a few people in the dance business, too." On second thought: "If they're still alive." She laughed. "Of course they are, alive and kicking up their heels. After seeing you dance the other night, I think it's high time you were introduced around, too."

Philip began to brighten. "Is that a promise?"

"Naturally, I'll expect you to escort me around town and see all the sights. Hell, boy, it's not only a promise—it's a threat."

Mikhail and Jennifer went to Aspen for a three-day honeymoon.

"Happy?" Mikhail asked as they sat in the ski lodge on a sofa in front of a roaring fire.

"Ecstatic! I'm glad it's off-season and we practically have the place to ourselves. All this lovemaking is liable to become a habit, and I won't want to taper off once we get back."

"Who said anything about tapering off?" Mikhail asked. He kissed her. "No way."

Jennifer stared into the fire as a serious expression came over her face. "You haven't been at the piano for four days."

"I'll get back to it once we return to Largo," Mikhail replied. "A break now and then is good for everyone. Actually, while you've been showering or doing the things you do by yourself, I've been sketching out a composition."

"You can do that without a piano?"

"Of course. I hear it in my head and write it down. It's a romance with a real lush love theme." He whistled part of it. "I heard it in my head after you fell asleep on our wedding night." He stood and reached his hand to her. "Come. There's a piano in the bar. I'll play it for you."

"Will they allow you?"

"If I ask real nicely," Mikhail said with a twinkle.

The bar was practically unoccupied. Mikhail asked the bartender's permission to play the piano. He kissed Jennifer and placed her on a stool at the piano bar. After a moment of gathering his thoughts, he began to play, improvising on the main melodic theme after initially stating it. By the time he reached the end, a small crowd had gathered around the piano and enthusiastically applauded him.

"My husband's a concert pianist," Jennifer said when he was asked to play popular songs.

A fake book was on the piano, and Mikhail obliged his audience by elaborating on several melodies he found in it. His performer's sense showed as he thrilled the listeners. He thought of old Mrs. Logan calling him an entertainer and laughed. "Granny Logan should see me now!"

"It was beautiful," Jennifer said when they left the bar nearly an hour later. "I mean the romance theme."

"You're right, it's only a theme now which I was improvising on," Mikhail replied, "but I know how I want to develop it. Good thing I didn't bring any music paper with me, or I'd be up half the night writing it down."

"I'm glad you have no paper." Jennifer grinned. "I want to be your piano tonight."

"Your wish is my command." Mikhail caught her in his arms as he carried her into the bedroom.

"I love you very much," Mikhail said before he placed her on the bed.

"And I love you more than words can say," Jennifer replied as she pulled him to her.

Once back at Largo, Mikhail continued to prove that he was a passionate, fulfilling lover; but Jennifer soon realized that he lacked the conventional ways of an ideal husband. The second night home, while she was preparing for bed, she heard piano music coming from the den. Upon investigation, she found Mikhail stark naked on the stool, feverishly playing through the music he had been sketching. She remained to listen for nearly fifteen minutes.

"Will you be long?" she asked.

"Not much longer," Mikhail rejoined. "Why don't you rest awhile? I'll be with you shortly."

Jennifer examined the clock as she stretched out on the bed to gather her thoughts. Ten-twenty. At twelve forty-five Mikhail climbed in bed beside her. She was sound asleep. He kissed her gently, put his arm around her and drifted off himself.

Mikhail required little sleep and he was always up bright and early, often working without dressing, a cup of black coffee nearby. After breakfast he would begin a marathon practice session for four to five hours without a break. Each afternoon he usually drove into Denver for a two-hour workout with Lionel Adams. Returning home midafternoon, he ritually swam for half an hour before he went back to the den for another hour or two at the piano.

Jennifer soon learned he did not like to be interrupted until dinnertime. Once she had put Mikhail's paint things into one part of the studio, where he had access to them should the urge strike, she arranged the remaining large area for her own use. In many ways it was an ideal situation for two artistically inclined people. She began to work early and continued until time to prepare a light lunch. Mikhail joined her, but he was usually preoccupied with thoughts of his work. Her afternoon was spent in the studio, unless she drove into Denver with him on days she had her own lessons.

"How's it going?" Vivian asked Jennifer three weeks after her wedding.

"Fine." She forced a smile. "I'm accomplishing all kinds of work, being extremely productive."

"From casual observation, I would guess the honeymoon was short-lived," Vivian speculated.

"Mikhail is terribly busy preparing for his concert. I've never seen a man drive himself as he does," Jennifer explained.

"Perhaps I should have warned you about that." Vivian smiled reassuringly. "His grandfather was that way, always on the go. I learned quickly that marriage is a partnership, but unless each individual goes his own way and does his own thing part of the time, it can lead to frustration. I had to let him know I was there and tried to be available for times together. If I had waited around for moments we could share intimately, I would have gone crazy. You must remember, he loves you dearly, but he has a lot at stake as far as his career is concerned."

"I realize that," Jennifer replied. "It's just taking a longer period of adjustment than I thought it would. I guess I read too many of those dreamy romance novels. I'm learning."

"Good." Vivian opened her purse. "I received a response to a letter of query I wrote to a publisher of children's books in your behalf." She fished it out. "They liked your drawings and have offered you a contract for fifteen illustrations for a text of a new book they're in the process of producing. At seventy-five bucks a picture, that could give you a bit of pin money."

"How wonderful!" Jennifer exclaimed as she scanned the letter and the accompanying contract. "What a fantastic surprise!" She threw her arms about Vivian.

"After I received this," Vivian continued, "I called an agent in New York whose name was given to me by a friend. I told him about the contract, and he was impressed enough to offer to see your work and possibly invite you to be represented by him."

"Oh, you're an angel!" Jennifer kissed her cheek.

"Not yet . . . but I'm working my way in that direction," Vivian quipped. "Incidentally, I'm open to an invitation to supper."

"Of course. I had intended to invite you." Jennifer clung to the older woman. "Come into the studio and see some of my latest work."

Mikhail arrived at Largo while Jennifer and Vivian were in the studio. He immediately went downstairs. When the women returned to the salon, Vivian noticed that Mikhail's car was parked next to hers.

"He always goes to the pool directly upon his return," Jennifer explained. "Sometimes I'm lucky enough to get a kiss in passing."

"Where's that pale blue number I left here?" Vivian asked. "I'll go down and give him a run for his money."

Jennifer found the bikini and puttered in the bedroom while Vivian changed.

"I won't win any Miss America contest," Vivian commented as she appeared, "but I'll play havoc with the judges at the Golden Age beauty pageant." Her figure was that of a woman half her age. "Just warn Philip, if he should show up, that I'm in the pool." She laughed on her way downstairs.

Jennifer did not have a chance to tell her that Philip had not been around as often as he had previously been.

Vivian had been in the water for two laps before Mikhail realized he was not swimming alone. He went to the shallow end and waited for her. Vivian swam to him for a greeting kiss.

"What're you doing here?" Mikhail asked.

"The same thing you are, but not as many," Vivian returned. "How much longer do you intend to splash around?"

Mikhail glanced up at the wall clock. "Ten minutes."

"Okay, I'll do a few more laps and tread water until you finish."

Ten minutes later, Mikhail floated up to where Vivian was sitting at the edge of the pool, dangling her feet in the water.

"What's on your mind?" Mikhail asked as he hoisted himself up to sit beside her.

"I want words with my favorite and only grandson, if you don't mind."

"Shoot." He reached for a towel to wrap around his shoulders.

"In the first place, short honeymoons are fine," Vivian stated, "but I'm convinced you have a lot to learn about women."

"Like what?"

"They can be made to feel that they're being neglected."

"I don't neglect Jenni."

"You certainly didn't even say boo when you arrived back from Denver," she said. "Just came down here and started your marathon bit. I know you're preoccupied with many things on your talented mind. You've got to learn to think first of Jenni and her feelings."

"Did she say she was upset?"

"She didn't have to. I could tell. She's not just a plaything, she's a woman who is deeply in love with you."

"And I'm deeply in love with her."

"Then, darn it, show her."

"I do!"

"Don't yell at me. I'm your grandmother, remember?"

"You don't let me forget," Mikhail said softly.

She took his hand. "I love Jenni, too. I just don't want to see anything come between you two to diminish the beautiful love I see in each of you. Try to find a little more time for her."

"Okay, I will. That's a promise. Anything else on your mind?" Mikhail asked as he put his arm around her.

"As a matter of fact, there is. Neglecting your wife is one thing, overlooking your friends is another matter."

"Now what?"

"I don't know whether you realize it or not, but you're practically a god to Philip. He worships you. Yesterday he confessed to me that he feels you don't want him around anymore."

"Not true. Okay, I've been lax there, too. I'll call him and make certain he comes out."

"I already invited him here this evening," Vivian said. "Being an artist with eccentric artistic attitudes is one thing, but neglecting those who love you is another. Find time—make time. Your grandfather did. All the success and triumph in the world will never replace love."

"I've got the message," he assured her and kissed her on the cheek. "I stand reprimanded."

"Forget your practice this afternoon and evening—take a partial holiday and be with us," Vivian said. "Go take your shower and get dressed. I'll shower and change upstairs."

Mikhail got to his feet and reached a hand to help her up.

Vivian put her hand to his face. "I love you, Mikhail, or I wouldn't say what I did."

"I know."

The evening was delightful. The four sat at the dining table and chatted until Philip said he would like to hear Mikhail's new composition. They adjourned to the den.

"That was absolutely fantastic!" Philip praised. "I love that theme melody. You know, what you should do is put some of your individual pieces together and let me come up with choreography for them."

"Do you think so?" Mikhail appeared impressed.

"Sure. Play it for me again." Philip leaned on the piano.

"That's our cue, Jenni, to clear the table and do up the dishes," Vivian suggested.

"Good idea."

"Wait," Philip said before Mikhail began to play again. "Record it on a cassette, and we'll take it downstairs and I'll show you."

"Okay." Mikhail rose from the piano stool and put on a tape. "I'll tell you when to turn it on."

"One thing you're going to have to learn, Jenni," Vivian said as she washed dishes and the other dried.

"What's that?"

"To force diversion on Mikhail. He's too much of a workhorse. Encourage him to have sessions like this with Philip and other of his friends. An extra hour or two of practice isn't going to make a difference. He's too much of a perfectionist—he's got to learn to let go and relax."

"Easier said than done."

"Not at all. I had quite a talk with him. He listened. You just have to remind him." Vivian dried her hands and hugged Jennifer. "Now I need another invitation."

"Like what?"

"To spend the night. I'm not up to driving back to Denver tonight."

"Of course. The guest room's yours," Jennifer said.

"And while you're issuing invitations, Philip could use one, too. You ask him."

Although they retired later than usual that night, Mikhail was more romantic and passionate than he had been in the past several days. Any doubts that Jennifer had had about their love were completely dispelled.

The next morning Mikhail was up early as usual, as were the others. Philip had a light breakfast and went to the basement studio to work out. Mikhail began practicing and Vivian prepared to leave.

"You look much better this morning, dearest Jenni," Vivian said when Jennifer walked her to the car.

"I feel better."

"You're going to have to assert yourself and become your own person."

"I'll try. Thanks for everything, Vivian."

"No—thank *you.* You were the perfect hostess."

Jennifer watched as Vivian's car drove down the road and out of sight. A chill was in the morning air, but she enjoyed the feel of it. She gathered a few twigs before she returned to the house and into the studio. With determination, she decided she definitely would become her own person. She thought of her mother and realized she definitely did not want to become like her, totally subjective and verging on being a nonentity. Prudence Logan could not help being the way she was, she had been raised like that. Jennifer would have her own career, her own success and, perhaps, her own notoriety.

CHAPTER TEN

Jennifer had perceived the trip to New York for the Carnegie Hall concert as a kind of second honeymoon. She realized that Mikhail would be busy part of the time, certainly spending long hours at practice, but she did not think that their hours together would be as limited as they turned out to be.

After the first day and evening by herself, Jennifer resolved to call the Barrus Agency, which Vivian had contacted from Denver, and set up an appointment to show her work. Surprisingly, she was invited to see Iris Barrus that afternoon at two-thirty.

"I'm abundantly impressed with your work," stately and stylishly dressed Iris Barrus commented after examining it. "You have talent in two directions. One, certainly as a creative painter, and secondly, as an illustrator. Your work is very commercial, and apparently you have a fairly rapid output. Both are qualities I like in my people."

"Thank you for saying so," Jennifer said as she studied the self-confident woman.

"Fortunately, you've arrived at an opportune time," Iris continued. "I'm in the process of negotiating for some textbook illustrations and possibly can assign fifty or more to you—if you wish to tackle the assignment."

"I would welcome it," Jennifer replied, smiling.

"The drawings would be of various sizes, and, of course, payment would vary accordingly. It's a very prominent company. I'll be able to get you as high as three hundred dollars for a full-page, four-color piece. They all will not be full pages."

"I'm most anxious to get established," Jennifer said. "The credits are more valuable to me than the money at this point."

"Good." Iris studied her a moment. "I see the ring. Is your husband with you here in New York?"

"Yes. He's a concert pianist, preparing for his Carnegie Hall debut next week. Naturally, he's busy at the piano most of the day, or handling other business matters, so I have a great deal of time to myself."

"How interesting. Then if I were to set up an appointment for you to see a designer at the publisher tomorrow, you'd be able to make it?"

"Definitely."

"They will want to see your work," Iris explained, "and if they're as impressed as I believe they will be, they'll show you the text and explain what is wanted. In that case, call me immediately and I'll work on the contract. In the meantime, I wish you to sign an exclusive representation agreement with me. If all goes well, I should have a definite commitment for you by next week."

Jennifer practically danced from the agent's office. She called the hotel on the faintest hope that Mikhail might be there. He was not. Nor was he there when she arrived back at five-thirty after window-shopping and buying a few odds and ends.

At nine-thirty, she received a call from Mikhail. "I'm still tied up with Cleo, honey. I may be another hour or so."

Jennifer watched television until eleven. She was in bed asleep by midnight. Mikhail arrived at one-thirty.

"Maybe it was a mistake for me to accompany you," Jennifer said the next morning. "Cleo Dennison seems to occupy most of your time."

"We've a lot to get settled before the concert." Mikhail tenderly kissed her. "Be patient, sweetheart, I know this is a difficult time for you—it's equally as difficult for me."

"I understand," Jennifer said, but she really did not.

"Aren't we going to have brunch together this morning?" Mikhail called from bed while Jennifer was busying in the bathroom.

"Can't. I've an eleven o'clock appointment with a publisher," she replied, "to show my work."

"I have to meet Cleo at one. We won't have time for lunch, and I may be tied up again tonight until late. Can you make your appointment for later?"

"No." Jennifer emerged from the bathroom wearing a pink suit with white accessories.

"Isn't that a bit gay for autumn—practically winter?" Mikhail asked as he observed her.

"I'll wear my maroon coat," she said. "It will give a bit of a somber cast to it. Besides, it's a bright sunny day."

Mikhail stood and caught her in a firm embrace. "I love you, Jenni." He kissed her and she responded for the moment.

"I love you, too," she replied. "However, as long as you're being productive in New York, I might as well be, too."

"I'm sorry about last night. Those things happen." Mikhail had a pleading sound to his voice.

"*What* things happen?"

"Late rehearsal, conversation over drinks with a few important people. I've got a lot riding on this concert."

"I'm certain you have." Jennifer kissed him again and eluded his hands as they reached to hug her. "And I have a lot riding on my appointment this morning, so I daren't be late."

"How important?"

"I'll tell you if it happens," Jennifer replied as she went for her coat. "Will we have dinner tonight?"

"I'll call you around four. If you should be out, I'll leave word." Mikhail stepped to her and helped her on with the coat. He kissed at the back of her neck. "Wish I had known about your appointment this morning."

"You would have had you been here before I went to sleep last night." Jennifer tried not to sound snappish. "Please don't mess me. I have to dash."

Mikhail turned her around and kissed her full on the mouth, hugging her tightly to him. "I promise I'll try to be back much earlier tonight."

Jennifer smiled, gathered her portfolio and purse. "Have a beautiful day, darling. I'll think about you."

Mikhail sat on the side of the bed and considered the situation before he rose and padded to the shower.

"Iris? Jennifer Alexander."

"How'd it go?"

"Perfect—or at least close to it. I just left. They gave me a copy of the layout specifications," Jennifer related. "Now they're waiting for your call."

"Fantastic! Get back to me in an hour or so," Iris instructed.

Jennifer wished she knew where she could reach Mikhail to tell him the news. Since she could not, she decided to shop for a less gay outfit, more in keeping with the season.

After speaking with Iris and receiving the welcome news, Jennifer returned to the hotel with her new acquisitions. She read through the publisher's specifications for illustrations until Mikhail called precisely at four.

"Sorry, sweetheart, I'm going to be busy probably until eight or nine. You'd better have dinner without me," Mikhail said. "I'm really upset about it."

"Do you think that Cleo is possibly detaining you so much for ulterior motives?" Jennifer dared to ask.

"What possible ulterior motives?"

"Your gorgeous body for starters."

"Don't be silly. She knows I'm married."

"That doesn't stop a designing woman," Jennifer said.

"I've told Cleo all about you. We've discussed the whole thing about our business relationship—and it's just that: business." Mikhail made an annoyed sound. "Come on, Jenni, don't think things like that."

"Sorry I mentioned it." Jennifer stretched on the bed. "I've wonderful news."

"Really? What?"

"Iris Barrus arranged for me to sign a contract for seventy-five pieces of illustrative artwork," Jennifer said gleefully. "I'll be practically independently wealthy—at least for a short while. Maybe I can buy that extra car we've been talking about."

"Hey, that's super news!" Mikhail cheered. "When do you start?"

"I'm reading through the specs now. If I'm fast and good, and the publisher accepts my work," Jennifer continued, "Iris is certain to have more for me almost immediately following. Isn't it exciting?"

"Yeah. Very." Mikhail's voice lacked enthusiasm. "If I get a break, I'll give you a call."

"Have fun, darling," Jennifer encouraged. Before he could object, she hung up.

The phone rang at five forty-five. Jennifer had napped for half an hour and was aroused from sleep. "Hello?"

"Jenni?"

"Yes."

"Philip Franklin."

"What are you doing calling me all the way from there?" she asked, still a bit groggy.

"All the way from where? You mean the lobby?" Philip laughed.

"Which lobby? Of this hotel?"

"Right. Got time for coffee or something?" he asked.

"Definitely. Give me ten minutes to get it together and I'll be right down."

"Okay, I'll be waiting."

What a pleasant surprise, Jennifer thought as she again slipped into the pink suit. Instead of wearing white shoes, she wore black and a coat to match.

"Hey, look at you!" Philip exclaimed. "What a knockout!"

"You're not so bad-looking yourself in your sporty three-piece suit," Jennifer returned. "Where shall we have coffee?"

"Somewhere elegant," Philip replied. "I feel in an extravagant mood."

"There's an interesting place across the street," Jennifer recommended, "and the coffee isn't cheap."

"Swell."

A brisk afternoon breeze swept down Seventh Avenue as they left the hotel. They hurried toward their destination.

"What brings you to New York?" Jennifer asked after they had ordered.

"A very grand lady, who happens to be doing her own thing this afternoon and evening," Philip answered with a twinkle.

"You have a girlfriend?"

"A ladyfriend—one we all know and love." Philip grinned.

"Vivian?"

"How'd you guess?"

"Who else? Don't think you're robbing the cradle, do you?" Jennifer joked.

"One of us may be—except it's all very platonic and above board." Philip laughed. "Gee, it's good to see you."

"You, too. I'm sorry you're otherwise occupied," Jennifer said after their coffee arrived. "Mikhail is busier than a cranberry merchant. I don't see much of him." She explained about her contract with the publisher.

"That's super, Jenni, really super!"

"If I hadn't had business of my own, I'd probably be upset," Jennifer said. "Mikhail did warn me to stay in Colorado until just a day or two before the concert. I knew he would be busy."

Philip stared into her eyes and put his hand to hers. "How's it really going, Jenni?"

"The contract is fantastic." Jennifer looked away.

"No—I mean with you and Mikhail."

"When we manage to have time together, it's beautiful."

"When you can manage?"

"I've just got to get my act together and learn to do my own thing." Jennifer forced a smile.

"Is that what you really want?" asked Philip as his fingers squeezed around hers.

"Naturally. I like the idea of being a liberated woman. After all, Mikhail and I can't play around all the time. He's involved in his work, I need to become absorbed in mine." Her eyes had become watery. She smiled bravely. "I'm really very much in love with Mikhail."

Philip looked down for a moment. "Since I have nothing planned for this evening, maybe you could have dinner with me. I'll even see if I can get tickets to a show."

Jennifer considered the invitation. "Okay, why not? Mikhail said he would be occupied until eight or nine—which probably means eleven or twelve. I think that would be great. Tell you what, I'll pay for the theater tickets, you do dinner. A deal?"

"If you say so." Philip brightened.

Jennifer left word at the hotel desk to tell her husband she had gone to dinner and the theater with a friend. When Mikhail called at seven-thirty to advise that he was going to be much later than he had speculated, he was given the message.

"What friend could she possibly be having dinner with?" Mikhail asked when he returned to where Cleo was waiting in the cocktail lounge.

"Maybe she's met someone. A lot of that goes on here in New York," Cleo said. "That kind of leaves you off the hook. We can have a leisurely supper with the Armbrusters."

"I doubt if I'll have much of an appetite."

Cleo put her hand to his. "I warned you it wouldn't be a hot idea to bring your wife here so early before the concert. Things have a way of happening."

Mikhail quickly finished his drink and waved for the waiter to order another.

"I loved the show," Philip said. "It's the first actual Broadway musical I've seen. I envied the dancers, even the chorus boys."

"It was a first for me, too," Jennifer remarked as they walked from the theater. "Shall we stop for hot chocolate or something?"

"Why not?" Philip held his arm for her to take. "Do you suppose Mikhail is back at the hotel yet? Maybe he could join us."

"Good idea." Jennifer stopped at a telephone booth and called. She was told there was no answer in their room.

"That upsets you, doesn't it?" Philip questioned as they sat at a booth in a restaurant. "I mean, Mikhail being out so late."

"I know he has to do what he has to do," Jennifer replied bravely. She gazed out the window.

"I have some good—well, at least interesting news," Philip said in an attempt to boost her spirits.

"Which is?" She turned back with a forced smile.

"I have an audition tomorrow. Vivian arranged it for me. I wasn't going to tell you until afterward—but I thought you'd be happy for me."

"I'll keep my fingers crossed." Jennifer made a valiant effort to be cheerful.

"And speaking of Vivian," Philip said, "I'd better not stay away from the hotel too late, or she'll worry about me."

"In that case we'd better drink up."

As they left the restaurant, Philip became quiet and somewhat withdrawn.

"Something on your mind?" Jennifer asked as they neared her hotel.

"I was just thinking—Mikhail and I have been good friends for a long time—since we were kids," Philip commented. "I'd just like you to know that if there's anything I can do to help you—I mean, like being around to listen when you need to talk—or whatever—that I'd really like to."

"Thanks for the offer. I'll remember it."

Jennifer apprehensively opened the hotel room door. Mikhail was not there. She tried to keep her thoughts positive, but shadows of doubt crept in. Undressed and ready for bed, she sat in a comfortable chair and watched flickering pictures on TV. She had almost fallen asleep when she heard the key turn in the door.

"Hi, honey," Mikhail said. "You still up and awake?" His words were slightly slurred. He kissed her, nearly losing his balance as he went to her. "I called several times. Guess you were out having a gay old time. I'm glad you did. I would have hated to think of you staying up in this gloomy room by yourself all the time."

"Looks like you've been having a gay old time, too," Jennifer returned, doing her best to control her anger.

"We had dinner at the Armbrusters."

"Whoever the Armbrusters may be."

"They're big patrons of Cleo's," Mikhail explained. "After calling several times and you weren't here, we stopped in a lounge for a couple of drinks. No big thing." He threw his jacket on the bed and pulled at his tie. "We just talked."

Jennifer stood. "Here, let me help you." She untied his tie as he kept trying for kisses. Then she unbuttoned his shirt. "Maybe you'd better take a shower."

"Yeah—maybe." Mikhail undressed and lurched into the bathroom. He was not completely dry when he returned and fell on the bed.

Jennifer rose from the chair where she had been seated and went to the bed to dry his back.

"Jenni, I'm sorry," he moaned, face down. "I guess I'm just caught up in all the excitement of the concert—and all this crazy way of life in the big city. I wish we were at Largo. I wish a lot of things."

Before she had him thoroughly dried off, he fell asleep. She managed to get him under the covers and tucked in. Ultimately, she crawled in beside him and kissed him on the cheek. Somehow she understood what he must be going through.

Jennifer was dressed and sitting at the desk going over the publisher's specs when Mikhail awakened the next morning. He felt on the bed beside him before he opened one eye and saw her. A pounding in his head kept him from rising quickly. "Hi, honey." He padded to where she was seated and kissed the top of her head.

"Feeling better this morning?" Jennifer asked cheerily.

"Not quite." He caressed her shoulders. "What're you doing up and all dressed?"

"Going over these papers. How about getting yourself together and taking me for breakfast?" Jennifer caught his hands, held them together and kissed them.

"Sure, I'd like that."

The hotel coffee shop was the most convenient. Mikhail was in better shape by the time he ordered breakfast.

"Look, I'm sorry about last night," he apologized.

"You've already told me that. I believe you."

"Yeah, I know—but it's been weird here," Mikhail said. "I wouldn't have drunk so much except—well, I was upset about you going out."

"You weren't available."

"I know—and I'm sorry about that, too." He drank coffee. "Who—or maybe it isn't any of my business."

"A mutual friend."

"Mutual? Who?"

"It was supposed to be a surprise," Jennifer said. "Philip Franklin took me out."

"Philip? Here in New York? Why didn't you say so?"

"I just did."

"I mean earlier. Hey, if I'd known that, I would have made an excuse with Cleo and joined you." Mikhail suddenly acted as if he had said the wrong thing.

"You could have made an excuse because of Philip," she questioned, "but not to be with me?"

"You know what I mean."

"No, I don't, Mikhail. What *do* you mean?"

He reached his hand across the table.

"The Armbrusters were so important you had to be with them last night?" Jennifer asked.

"Cleo insisted."

"Okay, leave it at that." Jennifer breathed deeply to regain control. "What are your plans for the rest of the day?"

Mikhail considered the question. "I'm going to cancel them and spend the day with you. We'll find something to do."

"No. Your concert's tomorrow night and you have to be ready for it."

"Come to the practice studio with me. I'll just run through the entire program once and we'll do something together," Mikhail pleaded.

Jennifer took the specs with her to go over while Mikhail practiced. She was aware he was not in his best form, but said nothing about it.

"Cleo was upset when I told her I couldn't make it tonight," Mikhail said. "I told her I was exhausted and needed the rest."

"If she really has your best interests at heart, it would seem that she would be more concerned about your physical condition," Jennifer commented. "Another night like last night and I doubt you'll make it through the concert."

"Okay, I've been foolish," Mikhail admitted. "There's no excuse for me drinking like I did. I just want to go home and be with you."

"Philip will probably call. He had an important audition today," Jennifer said as they arrived back at the hotel.

"I don't even want to talk to him—just want to be with you." Mikhail sounded like a pleading little boy.

They returned to their room and remained in bed until eight. Feeling hunger pains and in need of diversion, they went out for dinner.

CHAPTER ELEVEN

A night of rest and relaxation, intermingled with passionate exchange and romantic togetherness, put Mikhail in an excellent frame of mind the next day. Cleo called early to obtain his schedule and suggested that he practice in the late morning and plan to get adequate rest in the afternoon. She would expect him at Carnegie by seven.

"Want to come and hear me practice?" Mikhail asked after dressing casually in preparation to go to the Steinway rehearsal studios.

"I'd rather you did it on your own," Jennifer replied. "I want to do a little shopping for tonight. I'll meet you back here around four."

"Okay, if that's what you prefer." Mikhail hugged her tightly. "Hey, Mrs. Alexander, did I tell you I loved you today?"

"I lost count of the number of times." She kissed him affectionately.

Shortly after Mikhail left, Jennifer called the hotel where Philip was staying. "Hi," she said brightly. "Want to go shopping?"

"My plans anyway," Philip returned, "but with another lady."

"Maybe we can make it a threesome," Jennifer suggested.

"Fine with me. Here, I'll let you speak to the third party."

"Jenni? Vivian. How're you doing, honey? Philip told me the great news about your contract."

"I'm really excited."

"How'd the genius react to it?" Vivian asked.

"He thinks it's great. About shopping?"

"Need you ask? We'd love to have you along," Vivian said. "Lunch is on me. You didn't tell Mikhail I was here, did you?"

"I told him about going to the theater with Philip the night before last—nothing about you."

"Good. I see his picture up all over town," Vivian added. "At least his manager's doing well by him with publicity. There's even an article about his concert in today's *Times.* We'll talk about all that later. When and where shall we meet?"

Arrangements were made and Jennifer prepared to go out.

Carnegie Hall was not sold out. It was a good house considering that Mikhail was virtually unknown to New York audiences. Jennifer went backstage briefly to wish him luck. She excused herself when Cleo Dennison arrived. Returning to the auditorium, she was surprised to find Constance and Ivan Alexander in the company of her parents. Vivian, of course, was in the midst of them.

Clarence Logan had rented a tuxedo for the evening, which made him appear far more handsome than Jennifer had remembered seeing him. But her real shock was the transformation she beheld in her mother. Prudence Logan wore a chic emerald-green evening gown with a silver fox stole, pearls and sporting a stylish hairdo which made her seem years younger.

"I can't get over how beautiful you look, Mother," Jennifer exclaimed.

"I've Constance Alexander to thank for the alteration," Prudence confided. "The pearls are hers. We spent the entire day doing the beauty treatment while your father and father-in-law went off goodness knows where."

"Isn't she a knockout?" Vivian asked as she put her arm around Prudence. "I always knew she was a beauty like her daughter. She just had to do something about making it more noticeable."

Jennifer sat between her father and Philip, three fourths of the way back in the house. She held Philip's hand to control a case of nerves.

Mikhail received a polite ovation when he appeared. Gasps and whispers subsided before he turned to the piano, sat and took a few moments to prepare. His hands pounced on the keys as his body swayed majestically with his fiery interpretation of Chopin's Polonaise in A-flat. He performed stunningly. The technique shone flawless, the interpretation exhilarating, an echo of his intense creative genius. To watch him was a rare treat because he was every inch a showman, only slightly aware of his audience, and dramatically absorbed in the fantasies of the trance in which he had put himself.

The enthusiastic applause rang through the house for several minutes. He proudly, and with a touch of condescension, accepted the acclamation before he left the stage. A moment later he returned and sat down to play the major work on his program.

As he had done the first time Jennifer had heard him play, Mikhail seemed to be making love to the piano. Since she knew from personal experience, she was even more aware of his technique than anyone else. Ladies in the audience were duly impressed. Even most of the men became carried away with the splendor of his actions. He aroused tremendous excitement in practically everyone and lifted them to a frantic climax as his strong fingers found the final chords.

The audience rose as a unit with thunderous applause and a multitude of bravos. Hands ached and voices grew hoarse, calling him back again and again for bows.

"My word, I never realized what a tremendous pianist he is," Prudence exclaimed. "I've never experienced anything so electrifying."

"Nor I," Clarence added, rubbing his hands where they stung from clapping. "He's a brilliant performer!"

"He's okay, I guess, if you really like that sort of thing," Ivan Alexander admitted and reacted when his wife nudged him. "You know darn well, Constance, I'm not into all this artsy stuff. At least he plays loud, and that keeps me awake."

"Don't pay any attention to Ivan. He's as proud as he can be beneath his gruff facade," Constance explained. "He just likes to bluster, don't you, dear?"

"I could use a drink and wiggle my tail a little," Ivan muttered. "It's gone numb from all the sitting."

"Did you really like him, Mother?" Jennifer asked.

"I was overwhelmed. Such a passionate young man," Prudence said. "I mean that strictly in an artistic sense."

Jennifer hugged her mother. "I'm so glad you liked him. Too

bad Grandmother was such an old stick-in-the-mud and wouldn't come to hear him."

"She will one day," Vivian chimed. "I intend to see to it."

Mikhail began the second half of the program with Brahms's Rhapsody in E-flat. By then he had the audience completely in his control. He could do no wrong. His masterful performance was note-perfect, his interpretation brilliant and to watch him was thrilling. The cheering that followed was more that of a sports event than a classical concert.

Mikhail played Liszt for his last scheduled selection, again to unprecedented acclaim. When he was called back for the seventh time, he raised his hands and announced, "For an encore, I will play one of my original compositions, which I call 'Jennifer' and lovingly dedicated to the one who inspired it."

Cleo Dennison had suggested Debussy as an encore and had not been prepared for his announcement. Only after he began to play and she became aware of the tremendous reaction with which the audience received his composition, did she begin to unruffle her feathers a bit and relax. At the conclusion of the work, Mikhail was given another rousing standing ovation. He was called back again and again.

Never in Cleo's history of attending concerts had she heard such response for a virtually unknown musician. She went backstage before the applause had subsided and threw her arms about the young genius. "Fantastic! Absolutely thrilling, Mikhail! You couldn't have made me prouder."

"They really liked it, didn't they?" he said almost boyishly.

"I can't see what all the fuss is about," Ivan Alexander declared. "You hear one piano piece, you've heard them all."

Vivian elbowed him. "That's like saying you hear one car engine, you've heard them all. Don't be such a grouch."

"I can readily understand what all the excitement is about," Clarence Logan said. "I've heard a few good pianists in my time, but none to compare with my son-in-law—that is, Mikhail."

"He is your son-in-law," Prudence remarked, "and you should be rightly proud of him."

Constance put her arm about Prudence and hugged her. "Thanks for saying that. I expect that someday Ivan will regret not having been more supportive of Mikhail."

"Supportive, hell! I've given him everything," Ivan fumed. "Who's footed the bill for all of his studies and coaching sessions? I have."

"There are some things money can't buy, Ivan," Vivian inserted, "and show of affection is one of them."

Jennifer and Philip had hurried backstage. By the time they arrived, Mikhail was surrounded by a throng of admirers clamoring to endorse him with enthusiastic praise.

Cleo was in the midst of the melee, attempting to direct traffic and extending invitations to attend the reception afterward at the Plaza.

"Excuse me," Mikhail said as he pushed his way through the clustering bodies after spying Jennifer and Philip. When he managed to push his way through them, he ran to Jennifer and caught her in his arms, kissing her warmly and hugging with all his might. When he released her, he wrapped an encompassing bear hug around Philip and kissed him on the cheek. Finally, he put an arm around each of them. "My two favorite people in the entire world! We'll talk later." Another kiss to each and he dashed back into the crowd.

"We didn't get a chance to say a word," Philip complained.

"Never mind, there'll be time later," Jennifer replied. "He's in his glory now. Let him enjoy it."

Mikhail was surprised when he saw his parents, even more stunned when he finally recognized the Logans.

Nearly an hour later Cleo was able to clear everyone out and have a few moments with Mikhail in his dressing room. "You were more than I had anticipated you might be. I couldn't be more delighted."

"Thanks to you," Mikhail said. He held open his arms and she went to him. He hugged her tightly and kissed her on the cheek.

"Can't you do better than that?" Cleo asked.

Mikhail stared down into her admiring eyes before he kissed her lips. He reacted to her excited response before he gained control and curbed his enthusiasm. Slowly, he withdrew from her embrace. "It really did go well, didn't it?"

Cleo stood with arms folded as she watched him examine his reflection in the mirror. "The *Times* review should be out around midnight. I'm not certain about the others."

"What's the hurry in reading what the critics have to say? It's just their opinions anyway." Mikhail laughed as he gathered his things.

"I may have some very good news for you after tonight," Cleo said a short while later when they waited to catch a cab.

"Like what?"

"You'll see." Cleo took his arm.

"It's silly waiting around like this for a taxi," Mikhail said after three unsuccessful attempts at stopping a cab. "We could walk it faster."

"Why not?" Cleo was agreeable. "A late entrance is always fun."

"I was certainly pleased to see my folks and in-laws at the concert," Mikhail commented as they walked along Fifty-seventh Street. "I kind of figured my grandmother would show up —it's like her."

"She's footing the bill for this shindig at the Plaza, you know?" Cleo said.

"She is? Wow!" Mikhail thought a moment. "I thought the backers—"

"Don't tell her I told you. She didn't want you to know," Cleo related. "When do you anticipate returning to Denver?"

"In the next day or so, I hope," Mikhail replied.

"You hope?"

"The city's okay. I mean, I enjoy the excitement and all for a while," Mikhail said, "but I enjoy the solitude and quiet routine at home."

"Suppose I were to arrange for an extended concert tour for you?"

"That would be a different matter. I can adjust. But until such a time, I would just as soon stay in Colorado as much as I can. I should have taken you out to Largo. You'd see what I mean."

"Next time I'm in Denver." Cleo squeezed his arm.

The reception was a gala success. Once Mikhail arrived, he was constantly in demand, inundated with praise and accolades. He remained the center of attention throughout the night. When the newspapers were brought in with unanimous rave reviews about his performance, he was toasted and cheered, especially by his sponsors, who felt more than amply repaid for their support.

Philip and Jennifer remained until the end, but the rest of the family retired quite a bit earlier.

"Let's go somewhere for breakfast," Mikhail invited when the last of the guests had departed.

"You're crazy," Philip said.

"No, just hungry. I couldn't eat a thing all evening, but now I'm ravenous," Mikhail stated.

"Include me out," Cleo said as she watched Mikhail between Philip and Jennifer. "I've a big day tomorrow." She stepped forward and kissed Mikhail on the cheek. "Good show, Mikhail. Enjoy yourself." She turned to Jennifer. "You must be terribly proud of his accomplishments."

"I'm more than proud," Jennifer beamed.

"Give me a call tomorrow afternoon," Cleo said to Mikhail in parting.

They found an all-night restaurant after a little searching. Mikhail ordered a full meal; the other two had little appetite.

"Where do you go from here?" Philip asked as he sat across from the others.

"Funny you should ask," Mikhail smiled. "Apparently, there were some pretty big people in the music world present tonight. Cleo's working on a deal. She first wants to try for a solo-recital-type tour around the country with a lot of promo on it. Then she wants to set me up playing with various symphonies both in the U.S. and abroad. Isn't that fascinating?"

"Beautiful!" Philip exclaimed. His smile diminished as he observed Jennifer's reaction. "Hey, don't you think so, too?"

"It's very nice," Jennifer said unenthusiastically. "I suppose I'm going to have to learn to be the wife of a celebrity."

Mikhail put his arm around her. "Sure, you will. You have your artwork—the contracts and all—it would be easy to travel around. You can take your work with you."

"We'll see about that." Jennifer stifled a yawn. "When the time comes, we'll plan accordingly. I'm sorry. I'm exhausted. I think the concert was harder on me than it was on you. I'm emotionally drained. The only thing I can get excited about now is sleep."

Mikhail kissed her affectionately. "We'll go back to the hotel as soon as we're finished here."

When Mikhail called Cleo the next afternoon, she was bubbling with excitement. "You sound like you just won the lottery."

"Almost," Cleo replied. "Are you seated?"

"Sort of leaning."

"Then brace yourself, kiddo, I've got terrific news," Cleo said.

Mikhail adjusted his position. "Which is?"

"I have a fantastic five-month tour lined up for you right after the first of the year. Boston, Cleveland, Chicago, Los Angeles, just to name a few places. Nothing's concrete yet, but the enthusiasm about you is unbelievable. Booking people have been calling *me* . . . and not just for solo concerts. Some of the bigger, more prominent symphonies want you. You need to get at least four, maybe more, concertos under your belt—the big splashy kind that are favorites on symphonic programs. Two well-known orchestra conductors were at the concert last night. Word's got around."

"You're not just putting me on?" Mikhail asked. "I think I'm still dreaming."

"Well, pinch yourself awake, baby, this is no dream. Can we have dinner tonight to discuss the whole layout of what I'm working on?"

"I had promised Jenni—"

Jennifer had been listening to Mikhail's side of the conversation. She nodded her head to indicate that it was all right to change his plans.

"Just a sec." He put his hand over the phone. "Sure you won't mind?"

Jennifer braced herself and forced a pleasant smile. "Not if you have business to take care of. I understand."

Mikhail tried to read her expression and looked a question before he raised his hand. "Okay, Cleo, I can make it."

Mikhail crossed to where Jennifer was standing and took her in his arms. "Thank you, Jenni." He kissed her with compelling force.

"I knew when I first heard and saw you play," Jennifer said a while later as they reclined on the bed, "that you were an unusual talent and a man unlike all other men. I was even more aware of it after I got to know you. And when I agreed to marry you, I was well aware that it would not be a conventional type of relationship. I simply have to resign myself to certain facts and accept you as you are."

Mikhail kissed her and held her with all his might.

CHAPTER TWELVE

Since Mikhail had plans that night, Jennifer and Philip spent it on the town with her parents and in-laws, including Vivian. Philip remained in New York hoping that he would learn the result of his audition, while Vivian returned to Denver the following day with the Alexanders and the Logans.

Philip ultimately heard that his audition had been well received; however, the company had its quota of dancers for the remainder of the winter season. He was given encouragement and constructive suggestions about how he might be able to improve his chances of being accepted if he were to audition again in the spring.

"At least I tried it," Philip said as the three sat together on the flight back to Denver. "I need more gymnastic training for one thing. I never really thought of that as part of dance, but after seeing the company in rehearsals, I realize what they want. All the more challenge."

"Tell you what," Mikhail suggested, "I'll invest in some gymnastic equipment, a trampoline, that sort of thing, and put them in the basement studio. That way you can take lessons and come out to Largo and instruct me. Then when I go on tour, you can take care of the place while I'm gone."

"Great!" Philip exclaimed.

"Does that mean," Jennifer interrupted, a coldness in her voice, "that you're expecting me to travel with you on tour?"

"I had assumed—"

"Sweetheart, I love you," she said, "but I think you'd better try it on your own at first. I have my own work."

"You can't stay out at Largo by yourself," Mikhail objected.

"Maybe Vivian will come and stay with me," Jennifer suggested, "or—well, maybe someone else."

"I doubt if Vivian will want to be away from her friends and downtown activities," Mikhail said. "She might stay part of the time."

"And Philip will be coming out to practice," Jennifer added.

"I could even plan on spending a lot more time at Largo," Philip inserted. "I've finished school—only have my lessons privately and a class in dance a couple of times a week. My dad's supporting me. I'm certain if I explained the situation, he would agree to let me stay almost full-time at Largo."

Mikhail frowned. "Let me think about it."

Jennifer took his hand and applied pressure.

While there was a lot of family activity around the holidays, the last two months of the year found Mikhail in heavy, concentrated study. At the same time, Jennifer managed to fulfill her contracts, and Iris Barrus was busily setting up additional work for her.

Philip had all but moved in, commuting back and forth for his lessons, often going with Mikhail when he went in to work with Lionel Adams. For all three it was a very productive and basically a happy period. However, it turned out that both Mikhail and Jennifer spent more time with Philip than they did with each other. At times it seemed as if he had become a liaison between them.

The tour was set to begin the first week in February and Mikhail was convinced he was ready. The week prior to leaving Jennifer received a very large contract which she could not afford to refuse. She explained that she had been doing a lot of serious thinking about the situation and she believed it would be best if she remained at Largo.

"Okay, if that's what you want," Mikhail agreed. "I'll miss you, of course, but I will be busy much of the time and I know how lonely and neglected you felt in New York. It is extremely essential that I have a successful tour. In the future I can be more selective about the places I play, but while I'm getting established, I have to take whatever Cleo can book for me."

The last night before he left was one of the most beautiful that Jennifer and Mikhail had spent together, one that each would long remember.

Philip drove Mikhail to the airport the following day since it was an early morning flight, and he would remain in the city until afternoon with his lessons.

Jennifer went right to work after a prolonged farewell, and Mikhail promised to call every day. The new children's book she had contracted to illustrate was a fantasy, sort of pseudo science fiction for children, with one principal hero throughout. She planned to have Philip pose for her as a means of letting him pay his way.

Snow had fallen the night before, not heavy, but enough to cover the ground with a blanket of white. She stood at the window staring out for a long while before she finally got out her art materials and began to work. She tried not to think of Mikhail being gone for such a long period of time. It was difficult. She would fly to be with him from time to time, that had already been decided. Putting loneliness in the back of her mind, she determined to keep herself busy and enjoy being creative.

Several inches of snow fell during the first week Mikhail was away. The snowplowed road gave access to the main highway. Philip canceled lessons to avoid the arduous drive in such hazardous conditions. He practiced long hours and kept his body in tone by swimming. When Jennifer wanted him to pose, he obliged either in tights or a posing strap since the character she was drawing was to have an almost comic-book superhero appearance.

Long talks over quiet dinners or later in the den with a roaring fire provided opportunity for them to get to know each other better. They exchanged stories from childhood to present. Philip related many tales about Mikhail and how he had admired him over the years.

When Mikhail called, usually late at night, he always insisted on speaking with Philip. The concert tour was progressing very well. Cleo regularly flew in for the actual performances, but she had to return to New York between times to negotiate other business matters. Every time he called, he complained of loneliness and begged Jennifer to reconsider and come join him.

She explained that she was doing nicely on her current project, and if she finished ahead of schedule, she might try to spend some time with him. She missed him terribly and sincerely identified with his loneliness. Their conversations always ended with reaffirmation of their love and the tremendous desire they had for each other.

"I have to say," Jennifer remarked one night while they were sitting by the fire in the den, waiting for Mikhail's call, "that getting to know you and being with you is the closest I've ever felt to having a brother."

"Mikhail and I have been like brothers for as long as I can remember," Philip said. "He always stood up for me when I was a little kid and would whisk me away when the big guys tried to take advantage of me. I couldn't love him more if we were of the same flesh and blood."

"That's the sense of family I have about you, too."

Philip turned quiet and stared deeply into the fire. "I wonder if that's how I feel about you."

"You're not sure?"

"I have feelings, yes, I'm sure of that," Philip returned. "But I'm not certain how I can define these attitudes I have. I mean, we're here and together so much of the time—well, I sometimes have reactions toward you that aren't particularly brotherly—if you understand what I mean."

Jennifer scrutinized him with discernment. At times she had had to admit to herself that he had aroused sensual interest, especially while he was posing and she studied his body, not always with the detached eye of an artist. At times it took great effort on her part to remain objective.

"I've gone out with a few girls," Philip admitted when he looked away and tried to cover over what he had said. "Never was much of a ladies' man. I always figured I was too devoted to my dancing and preparing for a profession to become sidetracked with romantic notions. I envied Mikhail because he could concentrate on his art and still find time for—well—whatever. Maybe I just developed slower—you know, some guys do. Sometimes it makes me wonder what my real identity is."

Jennifer reached for his hand. "I understand what you're trying to say. In a sense I've been a late bloomer, too. I won't say it isn't frustrating being married to a man like Mikhail—it has been. Yet I know I'm very much in love with him and I'm a one-man person."

Philip squeezed her hand. "Jenni, do you *really* understand?"

"I believe so. And, when your big brother's away, if you can't confide in your sister, who can you confide in?" She smiled, but quickly had to glance away. "When I first saw the love between you and Mikhail, I didn't comprehend it. Once I realized what it actually was, I was deeply touched. I suppose I had developed a kind of love—at least a closeness to Pauline Maples, but it was never as profound as what I saw between Mikhail and you. Being an only child, I never had a sister or a brother—so I couldn't know how that kind of a sibling relationship could be. Now I want you to be my brother, too, a close, warm and loving brother."

Puzzling emotions surged through Philip. "Maybe I should go down and work out a little to deal with certain frustrations." He rose and stretched.

"Sounds like a good idea."

"Jenni—" Tears welled. He turned his head.

"You'll hear the phone when Mikhail calls. Naturally, he'll want to speak with you." Jennifer stared into the fire and looked up at him with an understanding smile.

"Sure—fine." Philip climbed from the sunken area of the room and dashed out.

Jennifer knew precisely what was troubling Philip. Funny, she thought, she never expected that he would develop that kind of an attachment. Maybe it was simply a phase he was going through, one which had to surface to be examined. He was intelligent. Feelings happen and physical reactions are stimulated.

When Mikhail called, he sounded as if he had been drinking. "Honey, I don't know how much longer I can go on without you. I miss you far more than you can possibly know."

"I miss you, too."

"I spend eight to ten hours a day practicing, find a gym somewhere with a pool—usually the YMCA—but I can't swim or exercise away my frustrations." Mikhail sounded as if he was on the verge of tears. "I need to be with you—to hold you—to touch you—to kiss you. Jenni, I'm ready to cancel the rest of the tour and come home."

"No, you mustn't do that—it means too much to you," Jennifer insisted. "Look, I should have all of the color prints finished by the end of the week—early to middle of next week at the latest. The rest are black-line. I can do those anywhere. Why don't I plan to fly out to be with you the week after next when you play with the Los Angeles Philharmonic?"

"For the rest of the tour?"

"I'm not certain about that. We'll have to take it one day at a time," Jennifer said thoughtfully.

"I need that—I need you with me, Jenni!"

"I want to be with you—more than I want anything else," she replied. She looked up to see Philip standing in the doorway. "You know I want only you."

Philip wore a forlorn expression before he lowered his head to hide it.

"What about Largo?" Mikhail asked. "Would you leave Philip alone?"

"I'm certain he can manage if he wants to stay by himself," Jennifer replied. "Or he can come and go as he chooses. Maybe he can find a friend who will stay with him. Is it really all that important?"

"No, not at all. So a few houseplants wither—they can always be replaced," Mikhail said. "Let me speak to Philip. Is he there?"

"Yes." She glanced up at the somber youth. "Mikhail wants to talk to you." Pause. "Philip?"

"I heard you. Just a sec." He breathed deeply before he crossed to the phone. "Hi, Mikhail. What's happening?"

"Who pulled your pigtail? You sound like you're in the depths of gloom?"

"No one. I've just been working out downstairs."

"This time of the night?"

"Something I had to deal with. Just catching my breath." He shot Jennifer a cautious look. "How's it going?"

"Lonely as hell. I miss you and Jenni."

"We miss you, too."

"Jenni says she's coming to be with me in a couple of weeks," Mikhail said. "Think you can manage there at Largo by yourself?"

"Sure. No problem."

"You must have a friend or two who would like to keep you company. After all, we'll be away until at least summer."

"I'll be okay—no problem." Philip tried to sound cheery. "Actually, I do have a friend. I'll see what I can arrange."

"Any word from New York?"

"Not yet."

Mikhail paused a moment. "Hey, what's wrong? I can hear something's bothering you."

"Nothing really." Philip glanced around. "Here, I'll give you back to Jenni."

"Philip?"

"Yeah?"

"Take care of yourself. Even when Jenni's with me, I'll call you regularly."

Philip handed the phone to Jennifer. "Think I'll shower and head for bed. Good night." He hurried from the den.

"What's with Philip?" Mikhail asked.

"I don't know. I didn't notice anything unusual until today," Jennifer replied. "We've kind of been snowed in for the last few days. He hasn't gone into Denver for any lessons."

"Sounds like a version of cabin fever," Mikhail guessed. "Encourage him to get out and around. The road to Largo is paved. If it's plowed, he shouldn't have any trouble driving it. Wish me well tomorrow night."

"You know I do," Jennifer said.

Long after Mikhail hung up, Jennifer sat staring at the fire. Had she agreed to fly to her husband because she wanted to be with him or because she was afraid of the closeness that was developing with Philip? No, she did want to be with Mikhail; she needed to feel his nearness, to touch and caress, to make love. Being independent was one thing, but she never wished to become so self-sufficient that she did not need him. As it occurred to her how deeply in love with him she was, all she could do was to think about finishing her work and join him as soon as she possibly could.

Before retiring, Jennifer thought again of Philip's strange reaction. She considered her feelings for him and she realized beyond a doubt that she had to be with Mikhail. She did not fear that something might happen, but she considered that it could.

Philip was a sensitive, creative person like Mikhail—and, for that matter, like herself. Emotions run deep and ultimately affect the imagination and the creative process.

Jennifer had photocopies made of her artwork and sent the color pieces to Iris Barrus in New York. She packed the copies to take with her along with a few basic art supplies. Others she could purchase when she needed them.

On the night before she was to leave for Los Angeles, Philip arrived at Largo with a friend, Andrew Yellen, who was a sculptor and an accomplished artist in his own right. Introduced by Vivian, Jennifer and Andrew had previously met at several art exhibits. Andrew immediately fell in love with Largo and offered to pay to be allowed to work there. Since Philip might have to fly to New York for another audition, it was arranged that Andrew would take care of the place in his absence, and otherwise he was free to share the facilities.

"Thanks for being understanding," Philip said at the airport after Jennifer had checked her baggage. "I appreciate all you've done for me."

"Both Mikhail and I appreciate you very much, Philip. And, naturally, we wish you all the best in whatever you may do." She kissed him and held him in a tight embrace for several seconds. "Take care of yourself and enjoy." She smiled as she pulled back. "I know you'll be successful."

"About all my silly emotions—"

"I understand that you have them. Only *you* can sort them out." Jennifer gave him another kiss before she picked up her hand luggage and went to the plane.

Jennifer thought often of Philip during the flight to Los Angeles, and she prayed that he would find happiness and all that he wanted to obtain out of life. It amused her to think that she was more familiar with the proportions of Philip's body than she was of Mikhail's. Maybe during the tour she would eventually be able to have her husband pose for her.

Mikhail was waiting for her at Los Angeles International Airport. When she saw him, Jennifer ran to him, dropping her cases and leaping into his embrace.

"Oh, I've missed you . . . missed you . . . missed you!"

Mikhail exclaimed as he kissed her and held her as closely to him as he possibly could.

"You can't know how much I've wanted to touch you like this," Jennifer returned.

In the cab ride to the hotel, Jennifer told him about Andrew Yellen and the arrangements she had made about Largo in case Philip had to fly to New York.

"Nothing is as important to me at this moment as being with you is," Mikhail said. "I trust your judgment—as well as Philip's. If you think Andrew Yellen is okay, I'm satisfied. I'm not even going to think about the Grieg Concerto until tomorrow when I rehearse with the orchestra. Tonight is ours and we're going to make the most of it."

At the hotel Mikhail left word that they were not to be disturbed under any circumstance.

"What if it's something important?" Jennifer asked on the way up in the elevator.

"Nothing is more important than being with you," Mikhail stated. "They'll take messages. I'll check them later. I just want to concentrate my time and energy on you."

Several hours later, after having had supper in their suite and spending romantic moments making up for lost time, Mikhail leaned back with his arm around Jennifer. "I really can't believe the reception I've had everywhere. I have to say this for Cleo, she's certainly handled things brilliantly. Next week San Francisco—and it's sold out. The following week in Seattle. Not sold out yet—but it's getting that way. And wait until you see what the critics have written about me. Even I can't believe it."

"I'm so very proud of you, my darling," Jennifer said as she ran her fingers over his face. "In a way, I'm glad we had the time apart. It gave me an opportunity to think and get my priorities straight."

"I hope I'm number one on your list."

"You always will be."

They kissed and the romantic cycle began again.

The Los Angeles performance was the most successful to date on the tour. Rave notices brought an invitation for Mikhail to return to play in the Hollywood Bowl that summer. He even had an offer to appear in a motion picture, which he declined since he had no aspirations to become an actor or to exploit his talents in that way—at least not for the present.

Mikhail attributed his West Coast triumph to the fact that Jennifer was with him.

"Okay, maybe her being here does make a difference," Cleo acknowledged somewhat reluctantly. "I have wires from Amsterdam, London and Vienna—to name a few. They all want me to set up dates for you to play. I thought I should ask before I booked you."

"I agreed to the five-month tour," Mikhail said, "and I'll honor my commitments. Afterward, however, I want to take a break, spend time at Largo and learn some new works. I can't go on playing the old war-horses forever. I need to expand my repertoire. Furthermore, I wish to include some of my own compositions."

"Your own compositions will come in time," Cleo said. "Okay, I'll put off the European tour for a while, but I do want you to think in terms of recording."

"I will—eventually."

Jennifer did not realize until after the San Francisco concert how much of a celebrity her husband had become. He did newspaper and radio interviews and appeared as a guest on television talk shows. His face had become well known and he was recognized wherever he went.

Mikhail's presence was wanted at parties, and he soon learned that he had to be selective with the ones he chose to attend. While he enjoyed the notoriety and the praise for his playing, he found that such social functions could be draining. Jennifer attended with him, but she felt out of place and often retired to the sidelines while the musical elite and patrons fawned over her husband. Women brazenly made advances toward him. Usually, by the end of the evening he would cling to Jennifer as a refuge from the overwhelming throng.

Jennifer kept in the background as much as possible and spent much time on her artwork, or sketching. When Mikhail was involved with interviews or rehearsals, she would sightsee or take in museums. By the time they reached Houston, she had completed her work project and sent the drawings to Iris Barrus, advising her that she was ready for another assignment whenever one was available.

Spring was evident when they arrived in St. Louis. Again Mikhail was obligated for the usual interviews and personal appearances. The all-important rehearsals with the orchestra consumed a large part of his time.

Two nights before the concert, after a grueling day, Mikhail showered and eagerly climbed into bed. Jennifer sighed and appeared exhausted. When he kissed her, she was noticeably less responsive than usual. Still, he was persuasive and they shared a romantic interlude.

"Something bothering you?" Mikhail asked later.

"Fatigue."

"You've had the entire day to yourself to relax," Mikhail stated. "I'm the one who should complain about fatigue. Are you upset about something?"

"The truth?"

"Yes. By all means."

"It was different before I finished my assignment," Jennifer related. "I had something definite to occupy my time. I called Iris today. She said she was working on another assignment, but nothing had materialized yet."

"Then come with me to the interviews—even to the rehearsals."

"No."

"Why?"

"I have a feeling of being on the sidelines, of being left out of the mainstream of what's happening," Jennifer explained. "I don't want the limelight, far from it."

"What do you want?"

"To pursue my own career," Jennifer said. "I want to be an artist, not just an artist's wife. I have to do my own thing. Maybe I should return to Largo. The weather will be nicer there now and I can get into my creative art—maybe study privately again. I feel like a fish out of water being unproductive."

"What about me?" Mikhail asked. "Don't you realize I need you with me? Even Cleo agrees that my performances are much better when you're with me. I'm a man. I need love and affection. I need you, Jenni."

"If the tour weren't stretched out over such a long time," she said, "it would be different."

"Can't you understand what this tour means to me? Don't you realize how important it is? I've had a healthy taste of it now—and it's in my blood. I'm like an addict, I want more and more and more—just as I've become addicted to you. I want more and more and more of you, too. I constantly decline propositions from all kinds of people because I desire only you."

"*All* kinds?"

"More than you can imagine. Do you know what it's like to be the center of that much attention? To have invitations thrust at me practically every day and to turn them down? I don't want them, that's the point, but it arouses me. Can you understand I absolutely need you with me?"

Jennifer remained quietly pondering his statements. "Yes, I can understand. Is that the only role you want me to play, just to be there at your beck and call, and isolate into oblivion like my mother has done all these years?"

"No. I don't want you to be like her. In the first place, I'm not like your father," Mikhail stated.

Jennifer turned over away from him. "I'm tired. Let's discuss this later. Please, Mikhail. I have a splitting headache. I just want to sleep."

Mikhail stared furiously at her for several moments before he pushed out of bed and pulled into his clothes.

"Where are you going?" Jennifer asked.

"Out!"

"Why? You need your rest."

"I have to think." Mikhail stormed for his topcoat. "I'll be back later."

It was only a little after midnight, Jennifer realized when she examined the clock. She thought it was much later. Because she had had difficulty sleeping the last few nights, she had purchased some over-the-counter sleeping pills. Two knocked her out. She did not regain consciousness when Mikhail returned sometime later.

Cleo had just arrived from New York, and attended the next day's rehearsal with the orchestra. Mikhail appeared to have difficulty from the beginning and twice asked to start over. After the first movement the conductor took him aside and Mikhail explained that he was just having a little trouble with preconcert nerves.

"We have to talk," Cleo said after Mikhail managed to get through a less than adequate rehearsal.

"I can't be perfect a hundred percent of the time," Mikhail stated. He forced a laugh. "You know what they say about lousy dress rehearsals."

"I know what they say," Cleo replied. "I also know what the conductor said, and I could see negative opinions in the faces of the orchestra members. What's the problem, Mikhail?"

"What problem?"

"My question." Cleo lit a cigarette. "Shall I guess, or do you want to tell me?"

"Just a little difference of opinion with Jenni last night," he replied. "I stayed out longer than I should have—and I probably had more to drink than I meant to have." He explained the situation.

That afternoon Cleo arranged to have a meeting with Jennifer.

"I'll come directly to the point, Jennifer," Cleo said, assuming a tough attitude. "Mikhail is a genius. I've handled a lot of concert performers and artists—I make a distinction. Mikhail is not only an artist but he has the potential of being a star of the first magnitude."

"I'm aware of his talent," Jennifer replied.

"I don't think you are—not completely," Cleo snapped. "I've had to hire another person in my office to handle calls and correspondence just about Mikhail. Word gets around fast in the music world. I turn down a dozen offers a week for him to play—or postpone them until I can work them in two or three years from now. And he hasn't even begun to record. After that I may have to have an entire staff devoted to him."

"I've never underestimated my husband's ability as a performer," Jennifer fired back. "I know he's good—better than good, excellent. However, I happen to be a creative person, too. I have my own career which is important to me. I'm bored silly sitting back in hotel rooms just waiting for an opportunity to spend a little time with him."

"You know, such an attitude is going to reflect in your private life," Cleo said calmly.

"Meaning?"

"Think about it. If you're not careful, Mikhail might turn in other directions for romantic gratification. He won't be the first man who's become discouraged with an uncooperative, unsympathetic wife. If you think your career is more important than his—"

"I didn't say it was more important—not in the overall scope of it," Jennifer returned, "but it is important to me."

"Then maybe you're the wrong sort of woman for him."

"How dare you?"

"Because I happen to be his manager and I am deeply concerned about his well-being and his state of mind," Cleo declared. "I'm not always of the opinion that a creative genius such as Mikhail should marry."

"Oh, I know he could nightly have his pick of anybody," Jennifer steamed. "Well, maybe that's what he should do—if that will make *you* happy!"

"Not me, Jennifer—Mikhail."

"Fine! Whoever!" Jennifer started to leave. "You tell him that! I really don't care!" She slammed the door when she left.

When Mikhail returned to the hotel room after an exhausting rehearsal, he discovered that many of Jennifer's personal things were gone, those that she could have carried in an overnight bag. He called downstairs to see if she had left word. None.

Mikhail's performance that night was adequate but far from sparkling. Technically perfect, his usual robust interpretation was lacking and his sense of showmanship was off.

"Have you seen or heard from Jennifer?" Mikhail asked Cleo when she joined him backstage.

"No." Cleo lit a cigarette and studied his distraught expression. "You claimed you couldn't play up to your usual standards before she joined you; yet I can see you're having more difficulty now that she's here."

"But she's not here! Don't you understand? I haven't seen her since I left the hotel this morning," Mikhail fumed.

"I have."

"When?"

"I had a lengthy conversation with her," Cleo recited, explaining what had been said. "There are certainly other women—"

"I don't want other women. I want Jenni!" Mikhail was in a rage. "How dare you say such things to her?"

"Because I happen to be your manager and I have a very personal interest in you." She put her hands to his chest.

Mikhail stared into her face before he grabbed her hands and pushed them aside. "Yes, there are other women I might find desirable, Cleo, but you're not one of them."

Cleo raised an eyebrow and folded her arms.

"From the moment I told you I was married," Mikhail said, "I've had the impression that you've been trying to come between Jennifer and me. I was naïve at first. I spent time with you over trivial matters when I should have been with her. Well, I'll tell you this, Cleo, if you interfere any further with my marriage, I'll drop you like a hot potato."

"We have a contract."

"Contracts are made to be broken," Mikhail flared. "You may not be aware of it, but I've had offers from some of the biggest managers in the business. I've felt a loyalty to you. But believe me, if anything happens between Jenni and me to break us up, it will also mean the end of my relationship with you."

"After all I've done for you?"

"Okay, so you've really helped me, made a lot of things possible, discovered me, etcetera," Mikhail said. "And I appreciate that. But I don't like you meddling in my private life. I've had conductors and music people tell me that it's unreal the exhaustive performance schedule you've put me through. Why? Because you wanted me to become an overnight sensation? Or because you wanted to tear Jenni and me apart?"

"Do you really believe that?"

"I don't know what to believe at this point," Mikhail stated. "Well, I haven't been as naïve as you thought I was. I was just stupid allowing you to twist me around. Now if you'll excuse me, I'm going out to look for Jenni!"

Mikhail was in bed, badly hungover, the next afternoon when Jennifer finally returned. He glanced up at her without realizing the time.

"Where've you been?" he asked.

"I took another hotel room," she said as she removed her outer things. "I had to put the pieces together."

Mikhail climbed from bed and went to her. "Oh, Jenni, I've missed you! I was worried sick about you." He tried to kiss her.

She held her hand in front of her mouth. "Your breath smells like the back end of a garbage truck."

"When I couldn't find you, I really tied one on. I'll go brush my teeth." He staggered somewhat as he went toward the bathroom.

"I called Iris Barrus this morning first thing," Jennifer said when he returned. "I told her if she couldn't keep me busy with work, I'd go to other free-lance agents. She made me promise I wouldn't do anything drastic for a couple of days. I know she'll come up with something. I've got to work, Mikhail. I have to do my own thing—it's the only way I'll be truly happy."

"Are you certain?"

"Positive. If I don't, I'll begin disliking you for forcing me exclusively into your lifestyle," she said. "I don't want that. You must do your thing and I must do mine. You see, I've had a taste of success, too—nothing to compare with yours—but in my own way I've accomplished something, and I like the feeling of that."

"Okay, okay, I'll agree to anything—just don't ever leave me again like you did last night," Mikhail begged.

"We were apart when I stayed at Largo."

"I know—and it nearly drove me crazy," Mikhail replied. "Shall I cancel the rest of the tour? Will that make you happy?"

"No."

"Do you want to return to Largo?"

"No, I don't think so. I want to wait and see what Iris comes up with," Jennifer stated. "If she can find something I can do to be constructive while I travel with you, that will be fine. If she locates a job where I need more equipment and space, then I will consider returning to Denver."

Mikhail braced himself against the back of a chair. "Jenni . . ."

Jennifer studied him a few moments before she resolutely crossed to him. She put her hands to his bare chest, rubbed them down and around to his back. "I also realized last night in that empty hotel room that I love you very much—and I don't want any other man but you. But, sweetheart, we've got to come to an agreement and a balance."

Mikhail quickly wrapped his arms around her. His mouth met hers with an all-consuming kiss.

That day and night their lovemaking was fantastic . . . *passion allegro.*

CHAPTER THIRTEEN

Mikhail's concert tour ended in late June after a concert in Washington, D.C. Cleo could have booked him through the summer, but he insisted he wanted his time free. With the exception of returning to Los Angeles to perform in the Hollywood Bowl in late July, he wanted at least the rest of the summer in Colorado to recuperate.

In the meantime, Philip had auditioned again in New York and was accepted to begin working with the company the first of October.

Fortunately, Jennifer had been kept busy with art assignments throughout the remainder of Mikhail's concert tour. While she attended the actual performances, she spent most of her time in creative endeavors and remained the attentive wife he wanted.

Once back at Largo, both Mikhail and Jennifer got into their old routines. When she had no contracts, Jennifer spent long hours at her creative art. She even found time to paint Mikhail's portrait.

Andrew Yellen had taken a cabin in the mountains, not too far away, so he regularly appeared to work out with Philip and Mikhail. Sometimes he would stay over, but Andrew was very much of a free spirit and he enjoyed being on his own.

By the end of August, although he sat long hours at the piano practicing or composing, Mikhail began to become restless. He worked regularly with Lionel Adams, increasing the time they spent together as he perfected new concert pieces.

Prior to the concert tour, there occasionally had been wine at Largo for dinner. Now Mikhail kept a liquor cabinet well stocked and insisted on having his two martinis each evening.

Neither Jennifer nor Philip cared for hard liquor, so Mikhail drank alone unless Andrew happened to be around.

"Something troubling you?" Vivian asked one afternoon when Mikhail stopped to see her after a three-hour session with Lionel.

"Why do you ask?" Mikhail tried for a congenial, relaxed attitude.

"Don't you think I know you pretty well after all these years?"

"I suppose there's a possibility of that." Mikhail laughed.

"Okay, fess up, what is it?" Vivian persisted.

"You know, when I first met Jenni's folks, her grandmother insisted on calling me an entertainer," he said after giving some thought to the question. "Of course, Grandmother Logan equated an entertainer with a showgirl or a strip-tease artist, or somebody like that. I was offended at the time."

"And since?"

"I've concluded that any performer who reacts to audience response is an entertainer of one sort or another," Mikhail admitted. "There's something about being up there, feeling the positive vibrations that come from an audience even before they applaud, that gets to you. Once they start applauding and cheering, some kind of magic happens inside. It tells me that all the years and hours of practice were worth it."

Vivian studied her grandson. "And you miss that, don't you?"

"That's the conclusion I'm beginning to reach."

"Beginning, my foot! It got in your system the first time you played a recital and, polite applause or not, you succumbed to it." Vivian took his hand. "Largo's a beautiful retreat for you to hide out at for a while, but you're in the allegro part of your life and you need to express it that way. I don't doubt you got bored with touring for five months—that would embalm anyone, living out of hotel rooms and restaurants. That was kind of like finger exercises for you. Now you should go for concerts spread apart so you can return to Largo in between. Let your manager book you to play every two or three months—not oftener. Go have your fling and get your ego fix from the audience, then come home and let your perking adrenaline carry you through other creative ventures before it begins to subside and you need another boost."

"Yeah, I'd like that."

"It would be best for both you and Jenni," Vivian continued. "Philip will be leaving in another month or two; you won't have him to fall back on. He's been good for both of you in many ways, but ultimately you two have to figure out how you're going to get along over the years of creative involvement balancing separate careers."

"I really dread Philip leaving. I guess I've used him somewhat as a crutch," Mikhail admitted.

"You both have. He's been good for you, and you've been good for him," Vivian stated. "But a man only needs a crutch when he believes he's a cripple. Your grandfather used to say that."

"Yeah."

"And don't you go letting Jenni become the crutch that Philip has been. No woman wants to be that. You have to stand on your own two feet and let her stand on hers. That's what it's all about."

"Both be independent?"

"Being independent will make you both more dependent on each other where it really counts," Vivian said. "If your grandfather hadn't been like that and made me self-sufficient, I might have fallen flat on my face when he died and never scampered back into a standing position. We each walked tall and depended on the support we received from our mutual love. Think about it, Mikhail, and be fair to both Jenni and yourself."

Later that day Mikhail called Cleo Dennison.

"I was wondering when I'd hear from you again," Cleo said. "In a way, I was hoping it would be before this—but I secretly knew it wouldn't be until you were ready. I've a calendar full of dates just waiting for you to give the go-ahead on."

"I'm not ready to be booked solid yet," Mikhail explained, "but I would like a concert or two in the relatively near future. I still need to relax and enjoy a little."

"Let me see what I can do. I'll be back to you later," Cleo said abruptly. "I've people here. I'll keep in touch."

The following day, while he was swimming, Cleo phoned. Philip took it and called Mikhail from the pool.

"I have an ideal situation for you and Jennifer," Cleo related.

"For both of us?"

"A chance to escape for a few weeks, more like a vacation than work," Cleo said. "The *Queen Elizabeth II* is sailing in two weeks for England. They need a pianist for the going and returning trip, one concert each way. In the meantime, the London Philharmonic would like you to solo with them while you're there. You can figure on six weeks. Five days crossing and five days return, a week in London rehearsing, and the rest of the time you'll be on vacation in England. How's that sound?"

"I will discuss it with Jenni and let you know. Okay?"

"Don't take too long. I need a commitment as soon as possible."

"Fine."

Mikhail swam fifteen minutes longer before he showered, dressed and went upstairs.

"Good news," Jennifer announced when she saw him. She had just come from gathering the mail.

"What is?" Mikhail asked as he hugged her.

"Iris has a new contract for me. A children's book," Jennifer said. "It pays well and I've six months to complete it. I should be finished with the oil landscape I've been working on in a couple of days."

"How would you like to go to London?"

"London—England?"

"Unless they've moved it." He related the conversation he had had with Cleo. "We'd have at least three weeks just to vacation."

Jennifer thought for a moment. "Okay. I like the idea. I can always do preliminary sketches while you're practicing for your concerts, and the rest of the time we can play tourist."

"You really do like the idea?"

"Why shouldn't I?" Jennifer asked.

"I thought maybe you'd had enough of the concert-tour business."

Jennifer laughed. "It won't be the same."

Mikhail called Cleo back and told her to set up the concerts.

She was pleased and promised to contact him in the next day or two.

A spark of excitement began to twinkle in Mikhail's eyes and he wore the look of anticipation that Jennifer recognized as being identical to that he had had prior to his concert tour. His attitude became boyish again and more playful.

"I can certainly tell you're anxious to go on the cruise," Jennifer said later that night when Mikhail's enthusiasm was demonstrated in a personal way.

"Well, maybe I can tell that you've got another assignment, too," Mikhail teased, "and not just because you told me so." He hugged and kissed her. "Oh, Jenni, I'm really looking forward to England—even if Cleo will be going along."

"Cleo?" A sharp coldness penetrated through Jennifer. "I hadn't realized."

"I didn't either—in the beginning. But I think it's great," he said. "You and Cleo should really make a concerted effort to get to know each other and become friends."

"Why?"

"For my sake," Mikhail replied simply. "I know there's been tension between you from the start. I can understand why."

"Why do you suppose there was tension?"

"Because Cleo knew you were in love with me," Mikhail said, "and she had a crush in the same direction."

"She did?"

"Couldn't you tell?" Mikhail laughed. "Her problem was that I was irrevocably in love with you and she didn't have a chance—no matter how hard she tried to win me away."

That icy sensation again jabbed at Jennifer's solar plexus. "Maybe I shouldn't go after all."

"Hey, what's that supposed to mean?"

"If Cleo's so hot for you, maybe I should just stay behind."

Mikhail wrapped his arms tightly around her. "Look, her attraction for me is one thing—neither you nor I can help that. My attraction is strictly for you, Mrs. Alexander, and don't you ever forget it." He kissed her. "Hey, come on, kiss back."

Jennifer stared into his eyes. "Okay." She kissed with all the love within her. "Better?"

"Much."

"In that case I'll accept the challenge," Jennifer said. "And if Cleo comes on to you—I'll give her a real run for her money."

"That's my girl."

They were soon so involved in each other that thoughts of Cleo were the last things on either of their minds.

Although there was still ample time before Philip had to move to New York, Mikhail made arrangements with Andrew Yellen to stay at Largo while they were on the cruise. Since Philip and Andrew got along so well together, there was no problem.

In her usual gregarious manner, Vivian insisted on giving a farewell party for Mikhail and Jennifer. Andrew and Philip were included among the guests.

Both Philip and Andrew drove Mikhail and Jennifer to the airport on the day of their departure.

"We'll have one night in New York," Mikhail explained to Andrew, "and the ship leaves tomorrow afternoon around five."

"I envy your trip," the somewhat bearish-appearing Andrew commented. "Maybe when you come back, you'll buy a few of my sculptures, then I'll be able to afford a trip abroad, too."

"We'll see." Mikhail patted him on the back. "Why don't you show your sculptures to Vivian? Maybe she can turn you on to some collectors."

"Good idea."

The four had a light breakfast at the airport and still had time to kill before the flight.

"I may try to rent one of those Village apartments," Philip said to fill in small talk while waiting. "Then maybe in time I can talk Andrew into coming to share it with me. That's where he should try to have his work shown."

"Right."

Once aboard the airliner and securely in their seats, Mikhail held Jennifer's hand. "Ever thought of living in New York?"

"It might be nice to have a second home there," Jennifer replied, "but I wouldn't want to live in New York all the time. Besides, I'd miss Largo."

"Good, because that's what I've been thinking about, too," Mikhail said, "having a place there as well as Largo."

"Sounds fascinating. I like the excitement of the city," Jennifer commented, "but I also love the tranquility at Largo."

After checking into a hotel in New York, Mikhail announced that he had tickets to the theater and plans to spend a special night on the town with his wife. "Furthermore, Cleo thinks we're flying in tomorrow morning, which means it's just you and me, Mrs. Alexander, and Manhattan."

"Funny, when we were here before," Jennifer said, "we never broke away from the concert routine and activities connected with it."

"I was too hung up preparing for my performances," replied Mikhail, "too excited about all that was happening with my career. Realistically, we were too fatigued from being on the road the second time to really enjoy ourselves."

The night proved to be one they would long remember—the theater, supper afterward and late night dancing. They arrived back at the hotel happily exhausted.

"Four o'clock in the morning?" Jennifer gasped, sagging as they returned to their hotel room.

"Is it that early? We can still go out for breakfast," he joked as he fell sprawled on the bed.

"Go ahead, but count me out." Jennifer began disrobing to punctuate her decision.

Later, as they snuggled close, Jennifer nearly asleep, Mikhail stroked her forehead and kissed her cheek. "I love you, Mrs. Alexander."

"I had a feeling you did."

Once checked aboard the *Queen Elizabeth II* and clothing hung, Mikhail excused himself to see if he could locate Cleo before sailing. Jennifer gratefully accepted the opportunity to relax and decide what she would wear to dinner and the first-night party. On her last trip to New York she had purchased two evening gowns, since prior to that she had never owned a formal. She chose a somewhat revealing dusty rose designer creation. The other, which was soft blue with a full skirt, she would save for the concert night. Her parents had presented her with a pearl necklace and earrings at the party which Vivian gave. For that afternoon she selected a simple beige suit with a chocolate blouse and an heirloom cameo which Grandmother Logan had given her.

"Cleo's only just arrived," Mikhail explained when he returned. "Aren't you all gussied up?"

"Like it?" Jennifer posed for him, slowly turning a complete circle.

"Elegant." He kissed her. "How would it be if I wore my light blue blazer and white pants?"

"A nice compliment to my outfit," Jennifer replied. "Which cabin is Cleo in?"

"Two down to your right."

"While you're changing, maybe I should start on my mission of détente and see if I can give her a hand," she suggested.

"Hey, that's a great idea." He caught her in a loving embrace and kissed her. "Thanks—I appreciate that. I'll stop by her stateroom when I'm ready. We'll all go to the bon voyage shindig together."

Jennifer breathed deeply before she knocked on Cleo's door.

"Why—Jennifer—" Cleo appeared surprised.

"I didn't bring a peace pipe, much less an olive branch," Jennifer said, "but I'd like to come in and maybe help you get situated."

Cleo stared curiously before she smiled and bade her enter.

As Jennifer stepped into the stateroom, a phrase flashed into her mind. *Agree with your adversaries quickly.* She smiled sweetly and made an attempt to exude her most persuasive charm.

Twenty-five minutes later Mikhail rapped at Cleo's door and she opened it to him.

"Departure is soon," Mikhail announced. "I'm certain Jenni will want to see it from above."

"Excellent idea," Cleo chimed. "Your wife's been helping me sort through a few things."

The three went to the upper deck, where they found places by the railing. A wonderfully warm day with crystal-clear skies made it an ideal time to sail. Jennifer was fascinated by the power of the tugboats, dwarfed by the mammoth ocean liner. They remained on deck past the tip of Manhattan Island and just beyond the Statue of Liberty. By then the ship's engines had taken over and the ocean breeze flapped at their clothing and hair.

"I need to find a ladies' room to repair the wind damage," Cleo declared as they went inside. "Why don't we meet you in the lounge in a few?"

Jennifer released Mikhail's hand to accompany Cleo.

Mikhail took time to check his appearance before entering the somewhat crowded lounge. He stood at the bar and ordered a drink.

"I know your face," a tall blond man with handsome features said as he turned to Mikhail beside him.

"Perhaps," Mikhail acknowledged.

"Reed Roberts," the man introduced himself. "Your first crossing?"

"Does it show?" He laughed. "I'm Mikhail Alexander."

"Sounds Russian and somewhat familiar."

"The family name used to be Alexandrov—and that's very Russian. Like the name, I'm a generation or two Americanized on one side—and God knows how long on the other. I take it you're a seasoned traveler, Mr. Roberts."

"I've made several crossings," Reed replied. "I'm traveling with my elderly father, who refuses to fly. Quite honestly, I enjoy these trips. We actually were going over a little later, but at the last minute Dad decided he wanted to travel at this time. Since I work with him, I'm available when he wants to go."

"Must be confining, traveling with your father," Mikhail commented as a means of small talk.

"Not at all. He knows many interesting people." Reed raised his glass to Mikhail. "Bon voyage—and all that good stuff."

"Likewise."

"You traveling alone, Mr. Alexander?"

"No—with my wife."

"Oh." Reed's smile diminished for a moment before it returned. "There are two kinds of travelers—those who are married and those who are not. Either way, I suppose it's an adventure of sorts. My father and I have separate staterooms. He does his thing and I do mine."

"Why did your father decide to make an earlier trip?"

"We're in the recording business. I deal more with modern and show-type music," Reed explained. "He's in the classical end—which, incidentally, is my preference, too. But someone has to handle the popular crap."

"How did that alter your father's plans?"

"He got word that a pianist is to play a concert aboard, and since he missed him when he played a while back in New York, he wants to see if all the fuss about him is valid."

"And he's making the trip just for that?" Mikhail asked incredulously.

Reed laughed. "Hardly. We have transatlantic interests."

"You're not married?"

Reed stared curiously into Mikhail's magnetic eyes. An enigmatic smile twisted at his lips. "No. Not recently."

They were interrupted by the arrival of Jennifer and Cleo. Mikhail made introductions.

"We really should go into the party," Cleo suggested. "The champagne's free there." She eyed Reed appraisingly. "Won't you join us?"

"A little later, thanks." Reed waved and turned back to the bar.

"Were you having some sort of game with him?" Cleo asked as they filed into the crowded ballroom where the party had been going on for some time.

"Meaning?"

"I recognized his name," Cleo said. "Obviously, his father is aboard to hear you play. Why didn't you come right out and tell him who you actually are?"

"Okay, so maybe it was a game of sorts," Mikhail replied as they went to mingle with the crowd. "Frankly, I'd rather be like any other tourist and enjoy a little anonymity while I can."

The handsome Alexanders were observed from all sides. People introduced themselves and chatted for a few moments before they were distracted.

"A little of this goes a long way," Jennifer commented after nearly an hour of being pushed against and jostled about.

"The problem is," Mikhail giddily explained, "they're drinking and you're not. One has to be a little high to get into this kind of thing."

"Okay, so I'm a party pooper," Jennifer admitted. "Wonder where Cleo's gone off to."

"She's excellent at mingling. She has it perfected to an art," Mikhail continued. "Has to have it for the line of work she's in. I know, you're perfectly content to be a shy little wallflower and express yourself in your painting and whatever. Frankly, I think you'd do well to push yourself forward a little more—not necessarily become ultragregarious, but at least be more outgoing."

"I've never been like that," Jennifer complained.

"I know. And it's high time you started to be."

"I'm a good listener," Jennifer said. "How about if we go up to the stateroom? All this noise and confusion is beginning to give me a headache."

"Ah, honey—"

"Okay, then why don't you remain here," Jennifer returned, "and I'll go to the cabin and take something for the pain? All this rocking of the ship is making me a little queasy."

"Can you find the way by yourself?" Mikhail asked.

"I'm certain I can," Jennifer replied, trying not to feel neglected.

Mikhail checked the time. "If you're not back in half an hour, I'll meet you in the stateroom. Okay?"

"Perfectly fine," Jennifer bit.

"Hey!" Mikhail caught her in a firm embrace and kissed her. "Okay, go. But feel better real soon. It's going to be a big night."

Shortly after Jennifer left, Cleo found her way to Mikhail. She had people for him to meet and did not seem to notice that Jennifer was no longer with him.

En route to the stateroom, Jennifer managed to lose her direction and wandered around until she asked directions. As she neared her destination, she had the distinct feeling that someone was following her. She stopped and glanced around.

"May I assist you, miss?" a distinguished-looking man with handsome features asked as he approached her. "I get the distinct impression that you're lost."

"I think I have the way now, thank you." She glanced a moment into his radiant eyes before she turned her head. "My stateroom should be down this way."

"It's easy to get turned around aboard ship." The man

beamed a suggestive smile and cultivated charm. "This is my third time aboard the *QE II* and I still have trouble getting my bearings. You're really quite lovely. May I know your name?"

"Mrs. Alexander," Jennifer replied.

"*Mrs.* Alexander?" he repeated. "I'm Devin Easterbrook. There isn't a Mrs. Easterbrook at the present time. Oh, you needn't be afraid of me. I'm just being friendly. It's expected aboard ship. We're all sort of like one big happy family."

Jennifer had to look away from his dynamic expression. "I just left my husband at the party. I'm feeling a little headachy and—"

"I've just the thing for you," Devin said as he reached into his pocket for a pill container. "Someone turned me on to these my first crossing, and I wouldn't make the trip without them. It's all this ship's motion that takes a bit of getting used to. One becomes a tad queasy and it brings on a slight headache."

Jennifer hesitantly took two of the pills from him.

"I'll find you some water. Wait here."

She observed that his stately figure moved with an air of authority and self-assurance. Her artistic eye perceived that he had interesting features and would probably make a fascinating subject to sketch. She wondered if she had the nerve to strike up a friendship with him without encouraging him in a romantic way. Why had that occurred to her?

"Here we go, lovely lady," Devin announced as he returned with a glass of water. "Why don't you just take this and we'll sit and chat for a few minutes while it takes effect. It's practically like magic and it works wonders. The ship's chemist will be open once we get out a ways. If they do the trick for you, you can purchase more. Or, better yet, you take mine and I'll replenish my supply later. I haven't had to use them at all this trip. Knock on wood." He laughed.

"I was headed for the stateroom."

"There's a little lounge area just around the bend," Devin explained. "Why don't we go there? Besides, having someone to talk with could well take your mind off your condition."

Jennifer managed to chuckle in agreement. "Okay. But I have to watch the time."

They found a comfortable sofa with maroon velvet covering that invited them to relax and stay awhile.

"Actually, I'm an Americanized Englishman," Devin said as he settled back. "I've done the international bit for years. I do business in the U.S., but I have a soft spot for the old homeland and all that sort of rot. I used to fly back and forth—it does save time, you know—but it's not near the fun. What line is your husband in?"

"He's a concert pianist."

"Oh, you're *that* Mrs. Alexander. How interesting." He produced a box of cigarettes and offered her one. "Do you care to join me?"

"Thank you, no, I don't smoke."

"Do you mind if I do?"

"Certainly not."

"You don't smoke," Devin commented as he exhaled, "or drink. I suppose you're also terribly faithful to your husband, too."

"Naturally."

"There's nothing natural about it," he returned. "It's a custom or a tradition, or whatever you wish to call it—but it's not natural in the least. If it were, a person would select one mate in the beginning without any shopping around, and that would be it. Even then, once connected with a mate, one's curiosity about the rest of the world doesn't stop there. Far from it. I always wonder at how people hypnotize themselves into believing that monogamy is such a sacred thing. It's a device which at one time, I suppose, served a purpose. Now it's as archaic as outdoor conveniences."

"I don't share your opinion," Jennifer replied, defending her beliefs.

"I take it you've been married under a year."

"How can you tell?"

"Oh my dear girl, there's still a glint of idealism in your eyes," Devin replied before he snuffed his cigarette. "Give yourself a little more time and you'll begin to think of a dalliance here and there."

An image of Philip Franklin flashed into her mind. She shook her head to erase it.

"You disagree? Of course you do." Devin studied her for a moment. "And what of your husband. Does he share your monogamistic views?"

"I believe he does."

"My dear, he's a human being. Unless he's highly religious and operates under the strict influence of a holy order, I doubt that he's all that puritanical in his thinking."

Jennifer considered the statement. "If you don't mind, I'd rather we changed the subject."

Devin patted her hand. "I bow to your wish, madame." He chuckled to himself. "Do you follow your husband around on his concert tours?"

"Sometimes."

"What do you do to occupy your time when you're not with him?"

"I'm an artist. I illustrate books—for one thing. I work in oils and watercolors on my creative endeavors," Jennifer replied. "Several of my paintings have been sold at galleries. My artwork consumes a lot of my time."

"I should imagine. I suppose it is an escape, too."

"Not when I do it commercially," Jennifer assured him.

"But as a child, you must have developed your interest during moments of escape," Devin persisted. "I suppose you've taken life-drawing classes and that sort of thing."

Again an image of Philip appeared in her mind, and she recalled how he self-consciously posed for her class at Larchmont the first time. "Yes."

"I've often thought it would be interesting," Devin said as he watched her. "To be a successful illustrator, one must have a fairly good awareness of human anatomy."

"True." She perceived where the conversation was leading. A glance at her watch, and she pushed herself forward. "I must get back to my stateroom. Mikhail will be returning."

"I envy your husband." Devin rose and gave her his hand.

Jennifer adjusted herself as she stood. "Oh? Do you aspire to be a concert pianist, too?"

Devin laughed loudly. "No, dear lady, not that. I envy him for having such a gorgeous creature with whom to express his romantic moments."

"Thank you."

Devin took the key from her. "Let me direct you, Mrs. Alexander. May I know your first name?"

"Jennifer."

"Oh, enchanting. It has a regal ring to it." Devin led the way. "You see, you were wandering down the wrong corridor all along."

When they arrived at the stateroom, Devin insisted on opening the door for her. "Thank you for a delightful chat. I'm certain we shall run into each other. There's no escaping the confines of the ship until we arrive in Southampton."

Jennifer shook his hand. "Thank you for your assistance."

"How's the head?"

"Much better. I'd forgotten about it."

"See! Didn't I tell you?" He handed her the pill container. "Be my guest, Jennifer."

"Thank you again. Now I must excuse myself." Jennifer stepped into the stateroom and closed the door firmly behind her. She leaned against the door for several seconds as she realized that it would have been relatively easy for her to have succumbed to his charms. She thought, too, of Andrew Yellen and how she had observed him with curious interest. Then she had rationalized her thoughts away by thinking that he might make an interesting subject to draw, quite the antithesis of slender, supple Philip Franklin.

Jennifer washed her face and touched up her makeup before Mikhail arrived. She kissed him.

"Darling, I appreciate your romantic enthusiasm," Mikhail said, showing the effects of what he had drunk, "but at this moment, I believe I am desperately in need of nourishment of the food kind. I should have sampled the goodies they were passing around. Whew!"

"Are you all right?"

"Fine—fine. Shall we dress for dinner, madame?"

Jennifer studied her husband as he began to peel out of his clothes. She caught his shirt and trousers before he dropped them.

"Jenni—I swear after tonight," Mikhail said after he had dressed and she was adjusting his tie, "there will be no more partying for me until after the concert. But tonight I want to pull out all the stops and enjoy."

"Whatever pleases you, my love," she replied condescendingly. "After all, this is our vacation . . . with a little work thrown in to make it interesting."

"I'm glad you understand."

"Fasten me." Jennifer turned her back to him.

"Hey, lady, you're going to knock eyes out in that little number." He patted her gently on the hindside. "Maybe we should skip dinner after all."

Jennifer pivoted around and kissed nibblingly at his lips. "No way, gorgeous gentleman." She straightened his lapels. "Shall we go."

"Only if you insist."

"I do." Another kiss before she wrapped a white knitted stole around her shoulders and led the way.

After dinner and a stroll around the deck, Jennifer had to take another of the pills Devin had given her.

"Where'd you get those?" Mikhail asked.

"These? Oh—the steward—when I returned to the stateroom." Why had she lied?

"Let me have a couple. I'm not seasick, but they may help my general fuzzy condition."

Cleo joined the Alexanders at the party that evening. She, too, appeared to be feeling little pain after imbibing as much as she had. "Tell you what—why don't we all mingle and dance with other people? Okay?"

"Fine with me," Jennifer replied.

"It is?" Mikhail asked.

"Why not? It's just a party and we might as well get acquainted," Jennifer said.

"Well, if anyone gets fresh with you—" Mikhail said.

"Oh, stop being so damned possessive," Cleo interrupted. "Let Jennifer have a little fun, too."

"Sounds like a conspiracy to me," he replied.

After a few drinks, Mikhail became uninhibited. He danced several dances with his wife and several more with Cleo before he began feeling his oats and asked other women to join him.

"Your husband's a very handsome man," Devin Easterbrook said as he came up behind Jennifer. "And he appears to be feeling little pain. Which is my cue to ask you to dance."

Jennifer turned with a scrutinizing smile. "I'd love to, Mr. Easterbrook."

"Devin," he corrected.

"Quite so." She laughed and allowed him to lead her to the dance floor.

CHAPTER FOURTEEN

Jennifer found Devin a graceful and debonair dancer, a man of charm and wit with an air of self-confidence. She guessed he was in his late thirties, from a cultured background, a world traveler and connoisseur of the arts. A humorous, positive, dynamic attitude made him pleasant company.

"No more for a while," Jennifer begged after four consecutive dances. "I'm not used to this."

"Perhaps a bit of fresh air?" Devin invited.

"That would be a welcome change."

He offered his arm and she took it.

"I enjoy dancing," Devin remarked as he led her to the outer deck, "especially when partnered with such a glamorous and exciting lady."

"I'd hardly call myself glamorous—and I'm not too sure about exciting."

"Let me assure you that it's true. You've a fresh beauty that attracts practically everyone's attention," he insisted. "Most men like to be seen with attractive ladies—I do. It has a remarkable way of boosting the male ego."

"I'm flattered."

"I'm honest." He studied her amused expression in the dim light that shone through the glass. "Do you intend to sketch while aboard?"

"I hope to spend some time on illustrations for a new book." Jennifer pulled the stole around her shoulders. "My husband will be devoting considerable time to preparation for the concert, so I'll be free to work. Being on the ocean has an element of inspiration."

"Not all work and no play, I trust."

"Oh no," Jennifer laughed gaily. "Mikhail promised not to

party again until after he plays the concert. I've honestly not seen him as uninhibited as he is tonight. I'm glad. He works hard and needs the diversion."

"And you?"

"Cleo—that's Mikhail's manager—suggested that it would be well for me to do my own thing, too. She thinks I cling too tightly to my husband."

"I've long embraced the theory that women lose men—or vice versa—if they cling too tenaciously." Devin lit a cigarette. "Perhaps you've become bored with your husband's concert tours because you've spent too much time waiting around for him and have not pursued your own interests."

"I've my artwork."

"Beyond that."

Jennifer considered the statement and concluded that she had designed her interests dutifully around Mikhail's—and she had been disappointed more than once. "Shall we go back to the party?"

"To check on your husband?"

"Not exactly."

"If you're chilly, why don't we stroll down below and have a look around?" Devin suggested.

"Shouldn't we get back?"

"Should we?"

Jennifer thought. "No." She turned to face him and smiled brightly. "I think it would be fun to go below."

"At your service, madame."

An hour passed before Mikhail began looking for his wife. He had created such a sensation with several attractive ladies that he had difficulty tearing himself away from their admiration. When he finally managed to elude them—feeling no pain and blurry-eyed—he lurched into the bar and ordered a drink. His thoughts had become fuzzy and distorted. He believed he was having fun, but had anyone asked him to describe how he felt—or to give his definition of *fun*—he would have had difficulty. Fun was subjective and he could only presume he had been enjoying himself.

"Well, well, I see you staggered back to square one," gregarious Reed Roberts remarked as he joined Mikhail.

Mikhail closed one eye to form a definitive impression before he recognized Roberts. "I seem to have misplaced my wife."

"That was a bit careless of you," Reed commented.

"No matter—she can't escape too far aboard ship."

"Quite so. But why would she want to escape?"

"Good question. I don't have a good answer." His eyes wandered vaguely over Reed's face before he smiled. "Maybe because we married prematurely—I mean, I still had some wild oats to sow and she—well, hell, Jenni had practically lived a sheltered existence—I mean, like cloistered—and she didn't have the chance to play around herself—you know." He threw a limp arm around Roberts' shoulders and leaned heavily against him. "Maybe Jenni needs to discover what she's missed by marrying so young. What do you think?"

"I think partying has begun to catch up with you," Roberts said sympathetically. "Booze has a way of loosening the tongue and bringing up thoughts from the subconscious that may have been neatly tucked away. Or it may bring forth desires that normally wouldn't surface."

"You mean like the desire to be possessive?"

"Possibly." Roberts watched as Mikhail made a poorly coordinated attempt to drink from the glass. "I must apologize for not recognizing your name when we first met." He scrutinized Mikhail appraisingly. "When I mentioned your name to my father at dinner, he told me who you are."

"Maybe I should check in the stateroom," Mikhail murmured, as if oblivious to Roberts' statement. "She had a headache earlier and may've retired."

"That's a possibility." Reed chuckled and patted him on the shoulder.

"I decided to marry in the first place," Mikhail confided a while later, after Reed bought them drinks, "because I had trouble with ladies throwing themselves at me—especially after they had heard me play. I like the attention—and I love my wife—unfortunately I've always been a free spirit and close confinement has been difficult for me to adjust to. I never thought I would become possessive of anyone."

"Is that why your wife travels with you—because you're possessive?"

"I suppose. Maybe I should try to find her."

"Want me to accompany you?"

"Why not? Maybe you can help me find my way."

"By all means," Reed said. He watched as Mikhail navigated with difficulty, then caught up with the pianist and placed a supporting arm about his shoulders. "Easy does it."

"Must be the boat rocking and pitching." Mikhail laughed.

"Could be."

Jennifer and Devin stopped in the second-class lounge and ordered sodas, which they shared at a quiet, isolated table.

"You don't drink, Devin?"

"Not anymore. Haven't in six years. With all my charm and debonair sophistication, I learned early on that I couldn't handle liquor—that my system was allergic to it," Devin related. "Once I accepted the fact and adjusted to it, I managed quite well in social circles without it. I don't miss it. And anyone who can't accept me as I am—well, that's their problem, not mine. I like to maintain control of my actions and remain aware of what I'm doing at all times."

"I rarely drink. I just don't like the taste—nor do I particularly enjoy the light-headedness that comes with it."

"It must be difficult for you to be married to a man like Mikhail Alexander, who obviously enjoys sloshing about in the stuff," Devin commented.

"I wonder if he does really enjoy it," Jennifer said. "Or if he just sloshes for the sake of sloshing."

Devin smiled. "You may have an excellent point there."

Jennifer and Devin returned to the ballroom a while later. By then the crowd had thinned and there was no sign of Mikhail or Cleo.

"Perhaps he's gone to the cabin," Devin suggested.

"Possibly. He *had* been overdoing it a bit."

"I'll walk you to your stateroom."

"Think I can find the way by myself."

"I insist, Jennifer. It's late and people have been partying excessively. For your own safety and protection, I think it would be best." He placed his hand at her elbow.

Jennifer became alarmed when she discovered Mikhail was not in the stateroom. "Guess all I can do is sit and wait."

"I suspect you do a lot of waiting for your husband, don't you?" Devin observed.

"I usually find something to occupy my time."

"Even when you're worried about where he may be or what he might be doing?"

"I try to detach."

"Successfully?"

Jennifer considered the question. "Sometimes." She forced a smile. "Thanks for everything, Devin—I've enjoyed your company."

"I would offer to wait with you," Devin said, "but your illustrious husband might return and mistake my intentions. In which case, I must thank you for your pleasurable company and conversation, Jennifer." He shook her hand but stared so intently into her fascinating face that it was all he could do to restrain himself from kissing her.

Jennifer's eyes sparkled in reaction until she turned her head and released his hand. "Goodnight."

Once Devin had departed, Jennifer examined her appearance, then stepped to Cleo's cabin, where she knocked several times. Finally Cleo appeared groggily.

"What is it?" Cleo asked, focusing with difficulty.

"Mikhail—I can't find him."

Cleo opened wide the door. "He's not here, kiddo—if that's where your suspicions are leading. I haven't seen him since I can't remember when. Don't worry—he'll show up. We'll talk tomorrow. Goodnight." She closed the door, leaving Jennifer with a perplexed expression.

Jennifer returned to the stateroom, removed her gown and prepared for bed. Seated in her nightie and peignoir, she resolved to wait up for Mikhail. The clocks were set an hour forward each night. It was two-thirty before she could hold her eyes open no longer and decided to stretch out on the bed. She soon fell asleep.

The fumbling sound of the key in the lock awakened Jennifer.

She examined the time: four-fifteen. When Mikhail could not unlock the door, she opened it for him. He was coatless, his shirttail outside his trousers. All in all, he appeared rumpled.

"Hi, honey—didn't wait up for me, did you?"

"No—I've been asleep for hours," Jennifer exaggerated.

"Me, too." He ripped open the buttons, tossed the shirt on the chair, kicked out of his shoes and peeled off his trousers. "Got a spike in my head." He gave her a half-hearted kiss and fell belly down on the bed.

"Mikhail?"

"Man, it was really some party," Mikhail mumbled before he lost consciousness.

"Mikhail? Sweetheart?" Jennifer rubbed her hand over his bare back. No response. She turned off the light and crawled in bed beside him.

Unable to immediately fall back asleep, confusing thoughts jammed through her mind. Mikhail had obviously drunk beyond his capacity. She had observed him drink in the past as if he had an unquenchable thirst. Others did not imbibe the way he did, not the so-called social drinkers. She wanted to think that he was just unwinding from the party and all, but she had begun to suspect that he was motivated by more significant reasons. What? Success? Notoriety? Suddenly receiving such admiration and acclaim for his genius at the piano? She thought of a motion picture she had seen on TV, *Too Much Too Soon*, and wondered if rapid escalation to stardom, as it were, was the case with her husband—and, in actuality, he was not emotionally or mentally ready to accept it—that it had all come too quickly and he could not fully cope with it—if at all.

Gently she rolled over next to him and let her hand run the length of his body, up and down, several times, with soothing caresses. She brushed her cheek against his bare shoulder and softly kissed it.

Neither Mikhail nor Jennifer awakened in time for breakfast the following morning, and they might have slept through lunch if the steward had not knocked at the door. Jennifer answered it. The steward presented her with Mikhail's coat and cummerbund.

"They simply called me from the cleaners to pick it up," the steward said. "It has been paid for."

Jennifer hung the coat and placed the cummerbund in a bureau drawer with Mikhail's underwear before she went to shower. When she emerged from the bathroom fifteen minutes later, Mikhail was sitting at the side of the bed, looking the worse for wear.

"I know we're at sea," Mikhail groaned, "but how many days have we been here?"

"One night," Jennifer said, wrapped in a large towel.

"Oh. What time did we get in last night?" he asked as he attempted to rise, but fell back down. "Wow! No more until after the concert. I swear it."

"You must have had a good time."

"I don't remember. I was hoping you could tell me." He managed to stand and lurched toward Jennifer. He caught her and tried for a kiss. She turned her head away. "Back end of a garbage truck, huh?"

"It's offensive."

"Yeah. I guess." He kissed her breast before he stumbled toward the bathroom. "See if you can get the steward to give you something for a hangover."

The shower was running when the steward brought the remedy.

"The last I recall, I was dancing with some foxy lady who claimed to be an actress," Mikhail explained when he emerged drying himself.

"A foxy actress?" Jennifer teased. "Open wide." She aimed the spoon with liquid toward his mouth.

"She could have been anything. In my condition anyone might have looked foxy." He made a face as he took the remedy. "What happened to the old fashioned plop-plop, fizz-fizz and goodies like that?"

"That's your chaser, darling." Jennifer handed him the glass with bubbling contents. "And after you danced with Miss Foxy?"

Mikhail eyed her over the glass and made another face, punctuated by a burp when he lowered it. "The rest of the night is a complete blank."

"Which means you might have spent quite a bit of time with Miss Foxy—either on the dance floor—or elsewhere."

Mikhail shrugged and belched again. "I just don't remember. I don't even recall coming to the cabin last night."

"This morning," Jennifer corrected.

"Whenever." He tried to penetrate her steel-cold expression.

"The steward brought your coat and cummerbund from the cleaners," Jennifer said and sucked in her cheeks. "Apparently you left them somewhere. Perhaps in Miss Foxy's stateroom."

He suddenly had the look of a little boy on the verge of tears. With effort he went to Jennifer and wrapped his arms around her. "Honey, I'm sorry. I don't know what happened. The way I feel now, I don't *ever* want another drink."

"Might be a good idea. You'd better get dressed. We both need lunch." Jennifer kissed him patronizingly. "Forget about last night. It's over. If you enjoyed yourself—fine."

Mikhail held her for several minutes before she pushed him away and went to dress.

Mikhail was not in the mood or pleasant physical condition to practice that day—far from it. Despite a throbbing head that would not quit and an all-over dissipated feeling, he dutifully spent four hours at the piano. Running through warm-up exercises was essential as well as going over the pieces he had selected to play for the ship's concert. Even his metaphysical trance did not help to alleviate the body discomfort, but it did aid him with the practicing. He vowed again that he would not touch another drop of liquor until after the concert performance.

Jennifer tried her best to shake out of the dismal mood brought on by the previous night's misadventures. She wanted to believe that Mikhail had simply passed out somewhere and had not been involved in any clandestine activity. She even wanted to think that he had blacked out early and had been unaware of anything that had happened afterward. Still there was the fact that his coat and cummerbund had been sent to the cleaners by some mysterious person.

The afternoon was beautifully clear and sunny. Jennifer took her sketchpad and pencils to the deck, where she found an unoccupied chaise longue. She drew three rudimentary pictures for the book she was illustrating. Her heart and mind were not in her work, so she soon set the project aside and acquiesced to the sun.

"Oh Devin," Jennifer exclaimed as if she had been startled, "it's you." He was standing above her, blocking the sun's rays.

"Mind if I join you, pretty lady?" Devin wore a pair of brief walking shorts and a form-fitting body shirt, which revealed that he was marvelously well built.

"Please do," she invited.

He sat on the chaise beside her and pointed to the sketchbook. "May I see?"

"Just a few rough drawings. I'm afraid they're not very inspired."

"Still upset about last night?" he asked as he studied her.

"Not necessarily upset."

"But not in the most positive state of mind either?"

"Is it that obvious?" she asked, shielding her eyes to observe his radiant expression.

"More an educated guess on my part," Devin laughed as he turned to examine the recent sketches and several others among the pages. "If these are without inspiration, I'd like to see your other work."

"I sometimes do as many as a dozen or more rough sketches before I decide on what I want to go for in the finished piece," she explained. "There's sometimes a drastic change—even in concept—from the first to the last rendering."

"I don't pretend to be an art critic," he commented, appraising the drawings, "far from it—but I'd judge that you have enormous talent, Jennifer, and you should take the backseat to no one . . . not even to your husband."

"Mikhail? My talent as an artist is nothing compared with his," she said. "He's the genius of the family."

"Don't place him on a pedestal too high, Jennifer," Devin warned. "And, for God's sake, don't underestimate your own talent."

"It's better to underestimate it and be surprised when it proves successful," she remarked, "than to overestimate it and be disappointed when it is not accepted."

"A fascinating theory. But then I find you a fascinating woman in many ways." Devin returned the sketchpad.

"A married woman, I must remind you." She leafed through the pages and avoided looking directly at him.

"Quite so, alas, quite so." Devin ran his eyes over her. "I wonder if your husband truly appreciates you—your beauty and your talent."

"My talent is not all that unusual—I mean for an artist. I simply have a good eye and the ability to record what I see. Mikhail is the creative genius. His artistry is far more refined than mine. I interpret visuals, he expresses from his soul."

"Such devoted admiration," Devin commented as he continued to observe her. "I prepared to go swimming. I've my bikini on beneath these walking shorts. I thought perhaps you might care to join me in the pool."

"Thanks for the invitation, but I'm really in a laid-back mood. Maybe tomorrow."

Devin skinned out of his shirt, watched for her reaction, and removed his shorts. He stretched, twisting from side to side, making soft ecstatic sounds as tension was released. "In that case, I'll settle for sun, too." The abbreviated bikini was hardly more than a string at the sides, almost as skimpy, Jennifer thought, as Philip's posing straps. His skin was nicely bronzed and, when he moved, it was difficult to tell where bikini covered him.

"You must sunbathe every day," Jennifer observed as she reached for her sketchpad and pencils. Her eyes followed his actions.

"Whenever possible," Devin replied. "I'm not your usual artist's-model type, but I believe I can hold a pose for an extended period of time if you want to have a go at it."

"You've nice proportions. I won't do a lot of detail. Okay, take a comfortable position." Jennifer began sketching.

"I must say," Devin remarked fifteen minutes later, "that it's quite a sensation having one's body so thoroughly scrutinized in such a detached manner. You *are* being objective, aren't you?"

"Strictly academic, I assure you."

"Is it?" He reached for the pad to examine her work. "I have to admit it looks like me—a bit flattering perhaps—but you've nicely captured my masculinity and some of my better attributes."

"An artist isn't like a camera," she said as she again examined the sketch, "which returns an exact likeness. An artist interprets what she sees, perhaps slightly distorts according to her own inner vision and perception."

"I see." Devin smiled and took another pose. "I kind of enjoy this."

Four sketches later and the afternoon breeze turning cool, Devin suggested tea. Jennifer agreed but wanted to stop in to see how Mikhail was faring, then go to her cabin to change clothes.

"Whatever makes you happy," Devin agreed as he hoisted into his walking shorts. "I suppose it wouldn't be enormously proper to take tea in such casual attire—not in public, that is. May I?" He reached for the sketchpad to examine before putting on his shirt. "My, my! I hadn't realized my bikini was so immodest or transparent. You certainly left no question concerning my manhood."

Jennifer smiled and gathered her things. "I'll meet you in half an hour at the lounge."

"I'll be looking forward to it with eager anticipation."

Still experiencing discomfort and not up to his usual enthusiasm, Mikhail practiced valiantly, going back over difficult passages until he perfected them. He acknowledged Jennifer's appearance with a preoccupied nod that indicated he did not wish to be disturbed. She understood, remained a few minutes to listen and quietly left.

She returned to the stateroom and changed into a white suit with a lavender scarf at her neck. Always stylishly handsome, she looked stunning in whatever she chose to wear. On her way to meet Devin, she attracted the admiring glances of many of the passengers.

"I know I've received attention," Jennifer said as she sat opposite Devin and tea was ordered, "still I rarely gave it second thought. Guess I've been too preoccupied in my own little creative world."

"Don't see how you could have possibly *not* noticed it."

"I didn't emerge from a world almost of another era until

after I met and married Mikhail," she explained. "I was walled in at a private girls' school where strict discipline was enforced. My parents' attitude was practically Victorian conservative as if they, too, were relics from another age. I'm certain my grandmother thought I would paint china teacups, which was the only reason she approved of my taking art courses. I presume they believed they would somehow chance on a man sympathetic to their ways of thinking and arrange for me to marry, therefore, remain in their world of isolation."

"You paint a dreary picture."

"I appreciate many of the values I've learned," she continued. "Yet when I evolved into a modern setting, I realized how inhibited I'd been. Once I'd experienced fulfillment with Mikhail, I no longer believed it was wrong to be a sensual person and set about to develop my individuality."

"How any person in this day and age could remain so closeted over those years is difficult for me to comprehend," Devin remarked. "I attended private schools, too—but we were all little hellions who experimented with every phase of life. Admittedly we defied discipline as often as possible, but sufficient rubbed off."

"You would have to know Larchmont—and my parents—to really comprehend what my sheltered childhood was like."

"Thank you very much, but no thank you, Jennifer." Devin smiled before he poured more tea.

"I don't wish to stay away too long. I want to be in the stateroom when Mikhail returns from practice."

"To be the dutiful wife?" he questioned with a sarcastic expression.

Jennifer thought a moment. "Yes. As a matter of fact, *yes.*"

Devin and Jennifer had several encounters in the next two days. She enjoyed chatting with him, but she was constantly aware of not letting down her guard or encouraging him in a sensual way. He continually made suggestive remarks and casually pressed against her with intimate overtones. Still he remained the essential gentleman and never did anything overtly to offend her.

True to his word, Mikhail did not imbibe anything stronger than sodas until after the concert.

By the third night aboard ship, most of the travelers had settled into a routine. The auditorium was adequately filled, considering that Mikhail was not yet a stellar attraction. However, those who did attend the concert were more than abundantly thrilled by the experience. Mikhail proved to be in excellent form and he played with a master's touch. His flamboyant performance, as usual, excited with provocative speculation. The response at the end was triumphant.

Throughout the concert, Jennifer sat trying to appear relaxed and not the least apprehensive. Devin, beside her, perceived that she was nervous for her husband. It was at that time, perhaps more than any other, that he realized how very devoted she was to Mikhail and, although she might be innocently flirtatious, she was not interested in Devin or any other man for anything but friendship. At first it bothered him, then he felt flattered that she did consider him a trusted friend.

Even with her concern for Mikhail, Jennifer was persistently aware of Devin's nearness and the aura of warmth that extended from him. She was delighted when he reacted with such acclamation to Mikhail's performance.

"I'm extremely happy for you, Jennifer," Devin exclaimed. "You have every reason to be proud of your husband. It has been a most enlightening experience."

When the crowd had thinned around Mikhail on stage, Jennifer tugged Devin forward to introduce them.

"Ah, the model!" Mikhail exclaimed. "Jenni's getting good, isn't she? I even recognized you with your clothes on." He laughed.

"You've seen my sketches of Devin?" she questioned.

"You were attempting to hide them from me, were you?"

"Of course not. I'm only surprised that you bothered to look at my work," she replied.

"I might surprise you in a lot of ways, my darling." Mikhail held her tightly and kissed her.

Devin slowly stepped back.

CHAPTER FIFTEEN

The reception following the concert proved to be nothing extraordinary: another shipboard party with the usual excessive drinking, pretentious mingling and forced hilarity. Mikhail remained cordial and graciously accepted the compliments directed toward him, yet he was not in a partying mood, nor did he react pleasantly to all the attention and accolades.

"Something wrong?" Cleo asked when she found a moment alone with him.

"The performance was exhausting and this party's so routine it verges on tedium." He laughed. "What is your candid opinion of my performance tonight?"

"As magnificent and exhilarating as ever."

"You're prejudiced." Mikhail laughed before his expression became serious. "I've been doing a lot of thinking the past few days, Cleo. First, I've reached the conclusion that I wish to spend the rest of the crossing in close company with my wife. Once we're in England, I'll devote sufficient time prior to the concert to practice; immediately following, however, I intend to take off for the next two weeks to be alone with Jenni. Interviews or anything you feel necessary, arrange before the performance. I will not be available until the return trip on the *QE II.*"

"Is something wrong?"

"Actually, something is right," Mikhail replied with a bright smile. "Now, do you see that man over there?" He pointed toward Devin Easterbrook.

"Yes. What about him?"

"I think it would be appropriate for you to get to know him," Mikhail suggested. "He's been spending time with Jenni—and, since I intend to occupy her time for the rest of the voyage, he probably will appreciate your company. Let's leave it at that."

Henry Roberts, prosperous-looking, portly and with an eye for talent, pushed his way to where Mikhail and Cleo were standing. His son, Reed, followed a short distance behind.

"I don't particularly like dealing with managers," Henry said after Cleo introduced herself. "I prefer going directly to the artist. Or, if I must use a liaison, I insist that the artist be present."

"What's the problem?" Mikhail questioned as he recognized Reed Roberts.

"Mikhail, this is my father, Henry Roberts," Reed introduced.

They shook hands as if preparing to square off for combat.

"I've an extravagant proposition for you, Mr. Alexander," the elder Roberts stated after expressing his praise concerning the performance. "I'm a producer of recordings and I'm impressed enough with your playing that I want to arrange to negotiate a deal. The project will take place over an extended period of time—but not without great advantage to you and your career."

"Really?" Mikhail laughed. "Cleo's my manager. I leave all that sort of thing to her. You deal with her and, if you come up with an interesting arrangement, I'll agree to it. Now, if you'll excuse me, the concert was wearing on me and I need to relax away from the excitement." He walked into a crowd of people and edged around them as his attention furtively remained on the Robertses and Cleo.

"He's certainly nonchalant," Henry commented.

"He's a creative artist, Mr. Roberts," Cleo replied. "And he's well aware of his worth and ability. Shall we discuss this tomorrow morning sometime around eleven? So good to have met you."

As Cleo left the somewhat gaping Robertses, Mikhail managed to maneuver into a position near the father and son where he was not observed.

"Thought you said you had the deal in the bag," Henry said to Reed. "Looks like there's no deal, much less a bag."

"He was agreeable the other night."

"When you had him plied with booze?" Henry asked. "That may work with your punk-rock or other popular-type performers, but not with genius."

"Okay, so I've a lot to learn, Dad," Reed admitted. "At least I tried."

"Maybe you should work on his wife," Henry suggested.

"Dad—"

"Okay, okay, I'll twist that manager around my little finger if it's the last thing I do," Henry declared and motioned for his son to follow him.

Mikhail considered what he had overheard and wondered precisely what the Robertses were trying to manipulate.

The following day Cleo reported to Mikhail that she had met with Henry Roberts and, quite frankly, she did not trust him, saying that he had made a proposition that was unsuitable to her —and left the matter at that.

True to his word, Mikhail hardly let Jennifer out of his sight the remainder of the voyage. They managed to avoid people—even Cleo—and spent much time in their stateroom, making up for the hours he had been occupied rehearsing for the concert. Yet, despite their wonderful moments together, Mikhail seemed anxious for the ship to dock.

"Did he come on to you?" Mikhail asked the last morning before debarkation, when he again examined the sketches Jennifer had drawn of Devin Easterbrook.

"Devin was always polite and very much a gentleman," she replied as she continued with last-minute packing. "He was there when I needed company while you were busy at the piano. I appreciated having someone with whom to talk. That's all."

Mikhail tried not to appear moody. It was not only Devin's attention to his wife that bothered him. He kept replaying over in his mind the conversation he had heard between Henry and Reed Roberts, and he wondered if Cleo had actually resolved the situation.

Shortly after exiting from the ship, both Mikhail's and Jennifer's spirits brightened when they saw Vivian and Philip waiting for them on the dock. They had flown over and rented a car to drive them to London. After lavish greetings, Mikhail and Philip went to gather luggage and Vivian superintended the operation. Jennifer lingered behind when she saw Devin Easterbrook approaching.

"I was hoping we'd have a moment to speak before you rushed off to the big city," Devin said. "Cleo and I have become acquainted, so I'm certain to see you the night of your husband's concert."

"Cleo?"

Devin smiled understandingly. "No doubt your husband put her up to it. That's fine. I find her interesting company."

"I'll look forward to seeing you again, Devin." She politely shook his hand, avoiding the dynamic gaze of his intense eyes. "Now you'll have to excuse me."

Devin watched as Jennifer hurried to join Mikhail and the others. "When one accepts singular missions in life, one must remain objective. Detach, Devin, detach!" he said to himself before he went to collect his own belongings.

Jennifer glanced back once. She had to admit fond feelings for Devin as a friend. She wanted to believe that she was not envious of his relationship with Cleo—whatever it might be. She hurried on and smiled as she approached her husband with Philip.

The following day Mikhail began dedicated practice for the London concert. Although Jennifer spent long sessions with Vivian and/or Philip, she had determined to devote the majority of that first week to finishing as many illustrations as possible in preparation for a fortnight of traveling through the English countryside and being alone with Mikhail.

"We must have conversation," Vivian said the second day when she managed to corner Mikhail in the hotel lobby.

"You know how busy I am."

"Too busy for a chat with your grandmother?"

"No, of course not. What's on your mind?"

"You—and Jennifer. Take me for a carriage ride."

Mikhail complied with her wishes, hailed a horse-drawn carriage in front of the hotel and ordered the driver to take them through Green Park.

"Okay, what's disturbing you?" he asked over the clip-clop rhythm of the horse's feet.

"I'm concerned about you," Vivian said, sitting back and breathing in autumn scents in the air on that gray day.

"How concerned?"

"Mikhail, you're a genius, a superb artist," she replied. "However, you may have a problem that could be destructive to your career."

"Which is?"

"I'll be blunt: excessive drinking."

"Has Jenni said something to you about it?"

"No. She wouldn't."

"Cleo?"

"As in the pot calling the kettle black? No. I rather imagine she would be the last person to say anything, unless it became a major concern." Vivian put her hand on his. "As you well know, your grandfather and I were extremely close all our lives—we had a kind of unspoken bond, which is not unusual with married people who devote their lives to each other. Since his passing, I have often dreamed about him—still do to this day. I believe he's always very close to me and sometimes I even sense that I feel his presence."

"What's this all leading to?" Mikhail asked with a laugh. "That Grandpa appeared to you in a dream and said that I was drinking excessively?"

"Almost that." Vivian stared into the intangible distance. "Your grandfather was a creative genius, too, an artist in his own right. As a young man, he discovered that his system was allergic to alcohol. It took him a while before he realized it; and, I confess, it was a rocky period for us before he did. Once he conquered his problem, what had been mediocre promise with his creative art became success and he sailed into his own realm of accomplishment."

"I didn't know that about him."

"Quite so. He was older than you are now when he discovered the source of his problem and took steps to do something about it," Vivian continued. "In any case, while you were on tour in the States, I had several vivid dreams about him—more than usual. You were included in one that was repeated. I would see him watching you play the piano and applauding your success."

Mikhail altered his position uneasily.

"Eventually, I realized he was trying to tell me something

about you," Vivian said, squeezing Mikhail's hand. "I felt he must be worried about some aspect of your life. So I hired someone to observe your actions while aboard the *Queen Elizabeth II.*"

"You did?" A worried expression crossed Mikhail's handsome features. "Who?"

"An old and dear friend. His identity is unimportant at this time—and it was well that you did not know who he is."

"You always did have a flair for mystery," Mikhail tried to joke. "Okay. So you received a negative report."

"Yes." Vivian glanced away from his smiling countenance. "I love you very much, Mikhail, maybe more than even you can know. And, because I do, I don't want you to jeopardize your career or your marriage."

"My marriage? Has Jenni—?"

"No. She loves you very much. Still I know she is deeply concerned about you and anxious that you succeed—and that your marriage succeeds. I trust a word to the wise will be sufficient."

Mikhail ruminated over Vivian's words when he practiced that day. He concluded that their talk had come at an auspicious time and he was deeply affected by it. He resolved to take steps to alter his life.

A message from Reed Roberts awaited Mikhail when he finished at the rehearsal hall, asking him to come to Roberts' suite at the Savoy that afternoon. Recalling the conversation he had overheard between Reed and his father the night of his ship concert, he decided it would be well to see what he wanted.

As he was leaving, Cleo stepped from a taxi. When she saw Mikhail, she asked the driver to wait. "I want to speak with you, Mikhail."

"If it's about Devin Easterbrook, you have my blessings," Mikhail said lightly as he read her angered expression.

"Far from that. I want to know when in the hell you signed an agreement with Henry Roberts."

"I never did."

"I've seen it, Mikhail. I know your signature," Cleo insisted.

"Impossible!" he stated. "Unless—" A fleeting picture shot into his mind. His hand went to his waist as if feeling for a cummerbund.

"Unless *what?*"

Mikhail thought a moment. "Something I must get to the bottom of. Mind dropping me at the Savoy?" He pushed her back into the taxi.

"We have a contract, Mikhail," Cleo stated.

"I know—I know." He almost added that contracts were often broken, but decided to hold his tongue. Another collage of pictures filtered into his mind, images that he did not care to discuss or reveal to Cleo.

Cleo let him out at the Savoy and ordered the driver to take her to her hotel.

Mikhail gathered his thoughts as he marched determinedly through the hotel lobby.

Clad in a silk robe, Reed Roberts opened the door to Mikhail. "Hello, Mikhail. I see you made it."

Mikhail entered and glanced around at the expensive suite.

"May I offer you a drink?" Reed asked.

"There's an agreement that I allegedly signed. I want it."

"My father has it."

Mikhail's strong fingers grabbed the front of Reed's robe and pulled him until they stood nose to nose. "I want that agreement . . . *now!*"

"I supposed that you would," Reed said coolly. "That's one reason I invited you here this evening." He looked down. "The silk wrinkles easily—if you don't mind. And, believe me, Mikhail, violence isn't necessary."

Mikhail released his hold. "Okay, explain."

"You don't recall signing it, do you?" Reed brushed the front of his robe. "The fact is, we came to a definite agreement that night."

"When I was intoxicated."

"You had had a few drinks."

"And you took advantage of the situation," Mikhail shouted.

"You can't remember what happened, because you had passed out on your feet. I think before you get too pugnacious, you should consider that I *do* know what occurred."

Mikhail took a firm stance. "Tell me."

"For one thing you became terribly sick and made a mess of your coat and cummerbund," Reed related. "I had to hold you over the toilet. You passed out after you signed the agreement. I had dozed but awakened when you eventually left my stateroom because of you banging the door behind you. I felt it was only polite to have your things cleaned and sent to you as quickly as possible."

"That's all that happened?"

"However, I do have a creative imagination, and if you intend to get nasty, I can fabricate a fabulous tale."

Again Mikhail charged at him.

Reed held out a restraining hand. "Don't be such a bull about it, Mikhail. Look at the bright side. I'll personally see that you receive the best possible contracts and that your records are produced in the highest quality. Do this for me. I'm bored with playing second fiddle to my father. You see, the contract was signed between you and me exclusively—*not* with my father."

"A contract for *what?*"

"Why, for me to produce records for you. I'm not in the position—nor are you—where I could fully manage your career. In time perhaps. And, at the present, it's best if I don't since you have a devoted manager. Once I heard you play, I was convinced of your prodigious talent. Okay, so I played a speck underhanded. It was my way of asserting myself."

"So you managed to get me drunk and had me sign?" Mikhail glared a moment before a chuckle began to bubble up from his abdomen. "Seriously, do you really think you can help me?"

"I'll make you my major project. By the time I've finished, the entire world will know about Mikhail Alexander and sing your praises. Give me this chance and you won't be sorry."

Mikhail considered the situation for a few moments, paced around the room and glanced out the window. "It's crazy—and I don't know how far you can be trusted."

"All the way, I assure you."

"But you know, I'm amused—and for some silly reason I want to have faith in you. Don't ask me why. Except I, too, have a father who tries to be overbearing. And I realize in this highly competitive business one needs all the assistance he can get to really be successful."

"I'll help all the way, Mikhail. Believe me, I'll be your devoted advocate."

"Sometimes I react on impulse. Okay, keep the agreement. I'll cover with Cleo on it. I warn you, however, if you don't come through with all you've promised, you had better consider going into hiding."

Reed extended his hand. "I'm sorry I had to be devious in my approach but—well, I wanted it . . . and drunk or sober, you're a hard man to bargain with."

Mikhail smiled and patted Reed's shoulder as he shook his hand. "Okay. We'll discuss details later. Oh, by the way, thanks for having the cleaning done."

As he left the hotel, Mikhail remembered part of the conversation he had had that first night aboard ship with Reed Roberts. Although it was fuzzy in memory, he did recall that Reed had offered to produce recordings and make arrangements for it to be accomplished with some of the biggest orchestras in the world. Furthermore, he promised to promote such records and work in conjunction with Cleo on other advancing aspects of his career.

Mikhail was able to handle Cleo and admitted that he had indeed signed with Reed Roberts to produce recordings. She would have to deal with him on her terms, but he assured her that Reed would work with her and could help him make gigantic steps as far as his career was concerned. Reluctantly, after a lot of persuasive conversation, she agreed to give it a try.

Reed Roberts proved that he had clout with the right people in the music business, particularly in London. By the night of the concert he had gathered a prominent group of influential patrons, the best critics and several representatives from recording companies to attend the performance in Albert Hall.

While the house was not completely full, the audience was significant, which was unusual for a relatively unknown artist despite the fact that he had played in major cities in the United States. Had Reed had more time, he could have managed greater hype and probably have filled the auditorium, but that would come later.

From the moment Mikhail walked onto the stage, his handsome appearance aroused the audience to excited response. He acknowledged their interest, nodded and went to the piano stool to prepare. The instant his fingers touched the keys with electric interpretation, he knew he had everyone in the palms of his hands. His performance was absolutely brilliant and the audience responded as no other had ever done.

The backstage area was mobbed at the conclusion of the performance. Mikhail had played three encores, all his own compositions. Reed Roberts embraced Mikhail and exclaimed that he wanted to see that Mikhail's own works were recorded. He foresaw great things in his future—they would discuss details at another time.

Cleo and Devin Easterbrook managed to congratulate Mikhail before the clamoring well-wishers arrived.

Jennifer and Philip stood on the sidelines, aware that there would be time later to lavish their praises on Mikhail. Vivian pushed her way through the crowd, hugged and kissed her grandson before she turned her attention away and went where Cleo and Devin were standing a short distance from the others. Out of the corner of his eye, Mikhail saw Vivian embrace Devin Easterbrook and, in a moment of perception, he realized that Devin was the friend she had sent to look into his behavior.

Jennifer, also, observed Vivian and Devin, and she, too, began to realize many things.

"Do you know Devin Easterbrook, that man with Vivian?" Jennifer asked.

"The three of us had lunch the other day," Philip replied. "They've known each other for years. You know Vivian, she likes to play her little games."

"Then it was no accident that Devin and I met."

Philip laughed. "I doubt that it was. Furthermore, I'll let you in on another secret, Reed Roberts is also an acquaintance of Vivian. We met him in New York and they seemed to be friends of long standing. I had dinner with Reed last night, and he's arranging for me to have an all-important audition with the Sadler's Wells ballet company. Like he said, it's not what you know or how much talent you have in this business that counts, but who you know—and who promotes you. And nobody knows that better than Vivian."

"So it seems." Jennifer forced a smile and decided that she

would make a point of getting better acquainted with Reed Roberts—but that would come in time.

"Darling, now the rest of the trip is for us to enjoy together," Mikhail said that night after they returned to their hotel room and began to prepare for bed. "I'll pick up a rental car first thing in the morning and we'll be off to see the British countryside. I thought we'd first go to Bath and eventually drive up the west coast."

"All of the rest of the trip—I mean, all the time?" Jennifer asked.

"Why? You got something going on the side?" Mikhail teased.

"No. But you know, I've been doing a lot of thinking about us," she said. "I love you very much, Mikhail, there should never be any question of that—"

"But—?"

"Vivian told me once that we should each have our independence and in that way we would be more dependent on each other's love," Jennifer replied.

"Sounds like Vivian." Stripped to his shorts, Mikhail padded into the bathroom to brush his teeth.

"I know we each agreed to do our own thing," she said as she stood at the door watching him, "at least as far as our work is concerned."

"So what's the problem?" he asked, words filtered through toothpaste.

"No problem."

"Why'd you bring it up if there wasn't?" Mikhail asked as he returned from the bathroom.

"I was thinking that you're becoming famous," she said, "and I'm beginning to grow up."

"I've always thought you were a big girl," Mikhail said as he wrapped his arms around her. "I like big girls."

"A lot of them?"

"Only one." He kissed her. "I'm making a resolution."

"About?"

"Getting serious about my career—all the way. And that means I've decided that alcohol has caused me to do some weird things in the past—and has interfered with my progress."

"Vivian?"

"How'd you guess?"

"Just a feeling I have."

He kissed her again. "Every day, I'm progressively more in love with you."

"And possessively?" she asked after another kiss.

"Possessively? I don't want you fooling around with other guys, if that's what you mean." He kissed about her neck and over her shoulders.

"Maybe I've been possessively in love with you." She responded to the vibrancy of his caresses and the exploring of his mouth.

"Okay. I don't fool around with any other women."

"I know that."

"In which case, let's drop it."

"No." She gently pushed him back. "We've gone through a period of adjustment, a time of really getting to know each other. I can't always follow you around like a puppy dog."

"Don't expect you to." He kissed her again and pushed his body fully against hers with obvious enthusiasm. "Jenni, Jenni, Jenni, I think maybe we've both finally grown up—a little."

"Meaning?"

"It's like with your sketches of Devin Easterbrook. He was an available model and you captured his likeness. Fine. It's a matter of trust and belief in one another. I can't keep other men from admiring you any more than you can stop women from turning on to me when they hear me play. But it's a matter of having faith in each other that will keep us from ever becoming possessive. You're a woman who has to make her place in the artistic world, just as I have to make mine. My little bird, I set you free —and if you fly back to me, I'll know you're mine."

Jennifer wrapped her arms firmly around him. "I'm here—I'm back to you right now—and I always will keep coming back for more—and more—and more!" She held her face to be kissed.

"Me, too." He kissed her and she returned it with all the creative energy within her. When he finally pulled his mouth from hers and gazed deeply into her eyes, he said, "I love you, Jennifer Alexander."

P08

"No more than I love you."
"Know what I want now?"
"Passion allegro?"
"Oh yes, indeed, *passion allegro!*"